"His memory has been affected."

The doctor's voice was carefully neutral.

"What do you mean? What has he forgotten?" Kelsey's eyes widened in dismay. How could Brandon have forgotten the time they'd spent in each other's arms?

The doctor lowered his voice. "Just one night. The night of the accident. He doesn't remember where he was going. He doesn't know why Douglas was following him." The doctor's eyes locked with hers. "And he doesn't have the faintest idea why you were in the car with him."

Kelsey moaned. "He doesn't remember?"

"No." The syllable was unforgiving. "And understand this—for some reason, Brandon finds it intolerable to remember that night. Rather than face it, his brain destroyed it. He doesn't know. And I don't want you to tell him."

KATHLEEN O'BRIEN, who lives in Florida, started out as a newspaper feature writer, but after marriage and motherhood, she traded that in to work on a novel. Kathleen likes strong heroes who overcome adversity, which is probably the result of her reading all those classic, tragic novels when she was younger. However, being a true romantic, she prefers *her* stories to end happily!

Books by Kathleen O'Brien

KATHLEEN O'BRIEN

A Forgotten Magic

Harlequin Books

TORONTO • NEW YORK • LONDON
AMSTERDAM • PARIS • SYDNEY • HAMBURG
STOCKHOLM • ATHENS • TOKYO • MILAN
MADRID • WARSAW • BUDAPEST • AUCKLAND

To Ann, Lori, Lyn and Terri for always being
there with a sympathetic ear or a swift kick and
most of all for the great gift of friendship.

ISBN 0-373-11642-X

A FORGOTTEN MAGIC

Copyright © 1994 by Kathleen O'Brien.

This edition published by arrangement with Harlequin Enterprises B. V.

® and TM are trademarks of the publisher. Trademarks indicated with
® are registered in the United States Patent and Trademark Office, the
Canadian Trade Marks Office and in other countries.

Printed in U.S.A.

CHAPTER ONE

THEY'D BEEN DRIVING for ten minutes in a mute, miserable purgatory of guilt. Ten minutes in a black silence that was not touched by the thunder, the frantic thrash of the wipers, or the pebble-hard raindrops that pelted the windshield.

Though Kelsey glanced from time to time at Brandon's profile, so stony that not even the strobe-flash of lightning could give it the illusion of movement, it didn't occur to her to speak to him. What was there to say?

More often she watched the speedometer. During each murky interval it seemed to leap upward, and every blink of lightning revealed a new, frighteningly high number. Was this his penance, she wondered, inviting fate to punish him? That wasn't like the Brandon Traherne she had come to love—not Douglas's fair-haired younger brother for whom all life was a grand game.

Maybe he was just trying to outrun the shame, trying to leave it behind at the Traherne mansion, which, if she turned around, she could still make out, though it was no more than an inky blot at the top of the cliff. But she didn't turn around. She didn't want to see it. Instead, she braided her fingers in her lap and stared at the mottled pattern of rain reflected on them, remembering how pale they'd looked against his skin. Had it been only minutes ago? Had those really been her fingers? Those boldly roaming fingers that had touched him everywhere....

The speedometer rose again, and her stomach dove down against her pelvis. It was mad to be going so fast in this weather, and she flicked another questioning glance at him.

She tried to will him to speak, but he didn't, not even by a flicker of those long eyelashes, betray any awareness of her. Was there, perhaps, a subtle whitening of his knuckles on the wheel? Surely the muscles in his right leg were tensing, as his foot pressed the gas pedal.

Oh, Brandon. Her fingers squeezed each other until they ached. Without his customary smile, he looked older, almost as old as Douglas, and harder, though never as hard as Douglas. And still he was gorgeous. His hair was wet, raked from his high brow in a perversely becoming disarray. Even now she wanted to touch it. Now—and always. Some uncontrollable part of her had wanted him from the first moment she'd seen him.

She forced her gaze away. Maybe, she told herself, using asperity to drive her thoughts into submission, maybe he was just in a hurry to be rid of her.

Without warning the car jolted, a sickening lunge to the side that defied all physical laws. Her own gasp, the sharp splintering of glass and a crunch of metal against metal simultaneously broke their silence.

"Jesus," Brandon hissed on a harsh intake of breath as the car rocked on its tires. Their headlights swung from the road to the trees and then, as Brandon fought the skid, back to the road again.

"Brandon, what...?" She turned toward him, too shocked to be frightened until she saw his face, whiter and grimmer than ever, his lips thin above a clenched jaw. Reaching for his arm, she fought the panic that rose in her. "What happened?"

Before he could answer, she saw the other car. Beyond Brandon's profile, a dark green sedan raced with them through the rain, its front bumper reflecting the glow of their taillights.

"What?" Her words had a razor edge of panic. "Who is it?"

"I think it's Douglas." Brandon's voice was deep, stunned as he pronounced his brother's name.

Douglas? Kelsey twisted in the seat. How did he know it was Douglas? She fixed her horrified stare on the other car. It was gaining on them, its nose now nearly up to Brandon's door. But the rain was too dense; the driver remained a shadow to her. She swallowed and tasted something bitter.

"Stop it, damn it!" Brandon yelled, and she knew he was calling to the man in the other car, though he never took his gaze from the road. "Are you crazy?"

But he was. He was. With a dreadful clarity, Kelsey knew it in an instant. Crazy with jealousy. She knew it even before the sedan swung into them, with another clash of metal, and they lurched again.

The edge of the cliff teased at their tires and, looking down, far, far down, she could see the whitecaps of the rain-whipped bay below them. She wanted to scream—the tension that had built up in her craved release—but she couldn't.

Then the lake disappeared, and the rumble of rocky earth under their tires told her they'd left the road, cutting away from the cliff. Brandon cursed as the other car clipped them again, catching their back fender, causing them to spin. There was no controlling the car now. Their headlights swept drunkenly across a jumble of tree trunks and tossing branches. Even Brandon wasn't strong enough to stop the mad spinning of the wheel.

Her last thought, as time slowed, was that she was glad she and Brandon had made love. As the raindrops parted and the thick brown trunk of a massive pine rushed toward them, the guilt that had been smothering her blew away, and she was *glad*. Glad her timid fingers had finally found courage, glad her body had known such pleasure, her heart such love, before all knowing ended.

She clutched at the dashboard as a rain-bowed branch caught the windshield, shattering it into a mosaic of glassy bits. Blood and rain ran down her cheeks, and she heard Brandon calling her. She turned her head to look at him, to answer him, but before she could find him the world exploded, and everything went black.

When she awoke, a lifetime later, Brandon was still calling her name.

"Kelsey." His voice was only a whisper now, almost lost in a bustle of strange voices and movement. People were hurrying all around her, and somewhere a mechanical voice was transmitting incoherent orders through a static haze. And yet she knew she was outside. She could hear, if she concentrated, sounds of the dying storm, the hollow plop of isolated raindrops, the far-off grumble of retreating thunder.

"Kelsey." Brandon's whisper found her through the noise, and the syllables tugged at her heart. He sounded fretful, confused. And he sounded faraway, as if he was drifting off on a boat he couldn't steer.

In her mind she answered him, sent a shapeless message of awareness, but she couldn't find the energy to utter actual words. The people around her were active, busy, noisy. Their bustle tired her, and she seemed to float helplessly in the center of it.

In a numb, disassociated way, she knew that someone was touching her, feeling her arms, gently squeezing and probing. But it wasn't Brandon. She knew Brandon's hands.

She tried to think, tried to remember why she was so afraid, why her head hurt so much, why some stranger would be touching her. But her thoughts were like a set of jacks scattered too wildly. She couldn't seem to scoop them up all at once.

"Kelsey!"

"Shh, now. She's fine." A woman's voice spoke from somewhere near Brandon's agitated whisper. It was a soothing voice. "We're checking her now. She'll be fine."

"Kelsey!" In spite of the comforting words, Brandon's whisper grew more intense. And then he groaned. "Oh, God, Kelsey."

"She's fine. You're both going to be fine," the woman repeated, her professionally consoling tone only serving to upset Kelsey. It reminded her of the day, twenty years ago, when a car had hit her dog. "He'll be fine, Kelsey, fine," the vet had promised. But her dog hadn't been fine. Her dog had died.

Kelsey moaned, surprising herself with the sound, as the probing hands moved to her legs. Why should that old memory return now? She wasn't going to die. Her head hurt, that was all. No one was going to die. No one.

"He can't hear you." A man's voice from directly over Kelsey's head broke through the woman's ongoing stream of comforting phrases. "He's out of it, poor guy."

The hands finally finished their inspection of her body, and Kelsey heard feet sloshing with heavy steps across the wet ground. "The lady's okay. Nothing broken. Lots of cuts—maybe a concussion. But we can move her. Get the stretcher."

Kelsey wanted to turn her head, wanted to look, but she couldn't control her muscles. Passively she allowed the strong hands to shift her onto the stretcher, and welcomed the warm, dry cloth they wrapped around her. Her head hurt less in this position, and as the stretcher rolled across the bumpy ground she let her eyes drift open.

Treetops jiggled against a cloudy night sky, as if she was watching film fed through an unsteady projector. A cool drop of rain loosened its hold on the tip of a leaf and fell onto her forehead. Her nostrils flared as she became aware of an incongruent smell. The smell of smoke. That didn't make sense. You couldn't have fire in the rain.

Suddenly frightened, she tried to look to the side, though the movement made her head hurt terribly. Brandon must be here somewhere. Why wasn't he calling her name? Those two syllables had been a lifeline, a focal point that kept her from being swept into the void she sensed at the edges of her brain.

Kelsey. Kelsey. Say my name, Brandon. Had they taken him away already? A bright light drove a shaft of pain into her eyes as they lifted her into an ambulance, and she squinted against it. Where was he? Why was he so quiet?

Brandon. She tossed her head restlessly, realizing the words came out merely as inarticulate moans. Someone was sitting next to her, pinching her arm. Why didn't they talk to her? Why didn't they tell her where he was? *Brandon.* She twitched in helpless agitation as she heard the ambulance's engine rev. No! Where was he? She wouldn't leave without him. She whimpered and tasted blood on her lips.

"Did that hurt?" The voice was beside her, and Kelsey sensed a shadow as someone leaned over, blocking out the interior light. "It's just an IV. It's routine, nothing to worry about."

Kelsey forced her eyes open a fraction, though the brightness still burned them. "Brandon," she said, forming the word as clearly as she could. It hurt to move her face at all. "Is he all right?"

The shadowed face was unreadable. "Brandon?" The woman, the same soothing paramedic who had been taking care of Brandon, spoke slowly. "Which one was Brandon?"

The woman had that voice again, the vet's voice, full of pain and false promises. In one terrible flash of understanding, Kelsey registered the woman's use of the past tense, and her lungs abruptly ceased to function. *No. No.* The light telescoped away from her, the woman's face growing small.

In vain, Kelsey tried to catch the escaping, shrinking light. How could the woman not know which one was Brandon? The two brothers were as different as sunshine and rain.

"Brandon," she murmured, her voice slurring and her eyes drifting shut. A new image floated in front of her, replacing the paramedic's worried frown. An image of Brandon laughing, his hazel eyes sparkling.

"Brandon," she said again, or at least she hoped she did. "He's the one who smiles."

She'd stored every one of his smiles in her memory, like sweet apples in a cellar—hoarded, almost, as if against a coming famine.

But she'd had such a short time. He was the glamorous, archaeologist brother who rarely returned to the family nest. She'd met him only a month ago, when, having heard about Douglas's engagement, he'd come home between digs, eager to offer congratulations, eager to meet the woman who would shortly be his sister-in-law.

A month's worth of smiles, each of which had seemed somehow to mark a stage of their relationship. The friendship that had grown silently, steadily, between them. The compelling physical attraction that had reached such a violent climax tonight.

At first he'd offered her polite smiles—the friendly, assessing smiles reserved for his brother's fiancée.

Then came the warmer smiles over dinner, when their eyes met in shared understanding of a silly joke, or one of Douglas's more pompous pronouncements.

Then sympathetic, as he helped her struggle with a stubborn computer in an effort to meet one of Douglas's unreasonable deadlines. Or grateful, when he watched her teach Ginny, his tomboyish little sister, to curl her hair.

Then shadowy and enigmatic, in the twilight, when they met unexpectedly in the garden, both damp and panting from an evening jog.

After that the smiles had grown self-conscious and stilted—when their hands touched over the dessert plates, when they brushed past one another in the garage, when they sat, side by side, watching television in the dark, the few inches between them prickling with awareness.

And, just in the past few days, came the smiles that were heavy with unexpressed, unwelcome feelings—forced smiles when he passed her bedroom door, saying good-night with uncomfortable formality, refusing to look below her neck, where her V-neck nightshirt dipped into the hollow between her breasts. And then, tonight, the smiles had ceased altogether, replaced by the grim, fierce surrender to passion...

"Brandon," she cried again as the ambulance sped away. But she knew he couldn't hear her. She had lost him, and his smiles, forever.

HOSPITALS LOOKED BETTER at night, Kelsey decided, when the lights were muted, softening the glare of whites and warming the icy gleam of metal. Besides, at night you saw it all with a tolerance born of painkillers and exhaustion.

This morning was a different story. The sunlight pushed aggressively through the uncurtained window, exposing every cold inch of the room, forcing her to face an utterly unfaceable reality. Fully dressed, Kelsey sat on the edge of her bed, brush forgotten in her palm, and stared at her shoes as though she'd never seen them before.

She hadn't seen them for more than two days. All that time she'd been lying in this bed, gowned and bandaged and grateful for the shot that came every four hours. Not that her physical pain was unendurable. *Lucky,* Dr. James had said blackly, as if she'd deliberately dodged her fair share of damage.

She had a few superficial cuts on her face and hands, some purpling bruises that had begun to look like tattoos, and a slight concussion that, in spite of the grand medical name, was no more than a bad headache. That was all.

No, the shots weren't for the injuries. They were to keep the other pains at bay, the hideous pains that circled her consciousness like snarling wolves.

Dr. James, a family friend who had always tended the Traherne children—Douglas, Brandon and then, much later, their unexpected but adored sister Ginny—had brought Kelsey the news that first night. He hadn't been able to keep his voice from shaking.

Douglas was dead.

That mad race through the rain had ended in tragedy. Douglas had lost control of his car, and it had toppled from the rain-slick cliff and fallen onto the rocks below, killing him on impact.

Dead. Staring at the doctor, Kelsey had tried to take it in, but she couldn't. Douglas, who had always seemed so invincible, so full of cruel power, was dead? It couldn't be. The doctor hadn't mentioned Brandon. Her stunned mind had grasped at this last straw of hope.

"What about . . . ?" She'd swallowed, an awkward, rasping movement, and tried again. "What about Brandon?"

Dr. James's face had grown harsh at the question, as though he thought she had no right to ask, but he gave the answer grimly, mincing no words. Brandon was alive, but he lay two floors down in the intensive-care unit, in an unnatural slumber that was the result of "intracranial bleeding." He might awaken in ten minutes—or never.

And his eyes... The blow to his head and the broken glass had done a lot of damage. Again, only time would tell how much. Right now the important thing was bringing him out of the coma.

She hadn't been permitted to see him. Unmoved by her pleas, Dr. James had refused to allow Kelsey into the ICU. She had wondered, looking at his tight mouth, whether he had taken some small satisfaction in being able to deny her that.

He held her responsible for all this tragedy; she knew that. He didn't ask her why she'd been in Brandon's car that night and not with Douglas. He didn't ask her why Douglas had been trying so wildly to catch them. But his suspicions and her guilt hung like a miasma in the room.

And so, denied the chance to see Brandon, she had lain here, awake in spite of the shots, her mind conjuring up images, each more horrible than the last, of Brandon lying alone, unaware, unreachable.

With trembling fingers she traced the zigzag of cuts along her hairline, wondering where the shards of glass had left their mark on Brandon. She fingered the tender lump above her temple, wondering whether, in his sleep, he felt the same throbbing ache. Did he dream? Did he know what had happened to him? And did he—oh, God—did he know about Douglas? Did he blame her, as Dr. James did? As she did herself?

That was the worst of all, a dizzying pain that made the room around her begin to tip and darken. The agony of knowing it was all her fault.

"Good news," Dr. James said, putting his ophthalmoscope into his pocket and scribbling on her chart. "Brandon has regained consciousness. He's not out of intensive care yet, but he's awake."

She looked up. Awake? The words sank in slowly, seeping through the layers of protective apathy under which she had buried herself.

And then a burst of hope. Conscious. Alive.

She sat abruptly erect, blood racing through her at breakneck speed. She stared at Dr. James's broad white back, trying to swallow the relieved sobs that clogged her throat.

"He's awake?" she managed. "He's going to be okay?"

Dr. James turned and gave her a long, steady look. It seemed to Kelsey that his gray eyes saw it all, her eagerness, her blood-flamed cheeks, her eyes that swam with foolish tears.

"We think so," he said guardedly. "He's better enough to make us feel a little more optimistic. He drifts in and out. That's normal—he's getting a lot of medication. And of course we're still worried about his eyes. But yes, he's definitely out of the coma."

He picked up his chart and headed toward the door. "Well, you look fine, ready to go. Do you have someone to pick you up, Miss Whit—"

Scrambling to her feet, which still felt shaky beneath her, Kelsey hurried to stop him before he left the room. She took his white coat in her fingers, ignoring the stab of pain from one of the small, unbandaged cuts.

"Please," she said, trying not to sound as desperate as she felt. "May I see him?"

"I really don't think it would be advisable. He shouldn't be disturbed—"

"I won't disturb him," she interrupted, still clutching his coat. She couldn't let go, not until he had said yes. "I just want to see him."

"He'll probably be asleep."

"I don't care." Her voice had a frantic sound, and she modulated it quickly. If he thought she was hysterical, he'd never let her go. "I'm not going to upset him."

"Well, I guess it's all right," he said grudgingly, as though his own capitulation surprised him. "But just for a minute. If he seems at all agitated, you must leave."

She nodded. "Of course."

His mind made up, Dr. James didn't waste any time. Motioning with his chart for her to follow him, he marched down the hall, white coat fluttering behind him. Kelsey followed, her feet steadier by the second.

It was still quite early, and they were the only people on the elevator. Dr. James stabbed the button for the fourth floor violently, as if he already regretted his decision.

"Before you go," he said, leaning against the wall as they waited for the sluggish doors to close. "You should be prepared. Brandon is—" he frowned and stabbed the button again "—pretty banged up. Much worse than you are."

Kelsey ran a hand self-consciously over the bandage on her jaw. "I know." Her heart twisted at the thought of Brandon's pain. "I understand. I'll be okay."

"I was thinking about Brandon," he said. "Brain injuries are tricky. The memory can be affected."

Her eyes widened in dismay. She hadn't even thought about this possibility. She hadn't thought beyond the prayer that Brandon would awaken and live. "Do you mean—" she took a deep breath and steadied herself against the wall "—that he may not remember me?"

The elevator jolted to a halt. "Oh, he remembers you quite clearly," Dr. James said as the doors wobbled open. "His long-term memory seems fine."

Relieved, Kelsey followed the doctor down the corridor, past the nurses' station. She didn't know how she could have stood it if Brandon had forgotten her. But she knew he couldn't have. Surely the time they'd spent in each other's arms was too potent to disappear.

Dr. James had stopped in front of a closed door. Her heartbeat danced nervously in her chest as she looked up at the doctor, waiting to see why he hesitated.

"As I said," he went on, blocking the doorway with his broad shoulders, "brain injuries are tricky. Sometimes they take away everything, sometimes just bits and pieces. In Brandon's case, the memory loss seems selective." He narrowed his eyes at Kelsey. "Disturbingly selective."

Bewildered, she met his accusatory gaze. "What do you mean? What has he forgotten?"

"Just a few hours." Dr. James lowered his voice, as if he feared the patients behind the closed doors could hear him. "Just one night. The night of the accident."

Kelsey gasped, bringing her damaged hands to her mouth.

"The whole night," Dr. James continued, his low voice insistent and somehow threatening. "He doesn't remember why he was leaving the house. He doesn't know why he was driving so fast. He doesn't know why Douglas was following him. He doesn't know how he lost control of the car."

The doctor's eyes locked with hers. "And he doesn't have the faintest idea why you were in the car with him."

Kelsey moaned. She let her head droop against the wall, suddenly drained of the strength to hold it up. "He doesn't remember?"

"No." The syllable was unforgiving. "And understand this, Miss Whittaker. I don't know what happened that night, either. I only know that, for some reason, Brandon finds it intolerable to remember. Rather than face it, his brain has destroyed it. He doesn't know. And I don't want you to tell him.''

BRANDON WELCOMED the numbness that crept across his prone body like a slow shadow. The medicine had finally kicked in again, thank heaven.

The nurse was still chattering, but her voice began to fade as Brandon let the medicine world close over him, sucking him down into a place of meaningless color, sound and sensation. The ache in his head, fierce a moment ago, was now just a blackness that had the low throb of a cello. The stabbing in his eyes was merely a distant red whine.

Strange, though, he thought with spreading detachment, that he, who had always loved life, pain and all, should now prefer this empty unreality.

But never before had his world been like this—full of people who wanted to ask him unanswerable questions and tell him unbearable things. Not so strange, then. Who wouldn't flee from such a world? He let every muscle go limp, encouraging the void to take him.

Before he had made complete his escape, he heard footsteps approaching his bed. The noise snagged him, slowing his descent.

''Brandon.'' A soft voice was trying to find him. A beautiful voice, but desperate—a single match struggling to illuminate a bottomless well. ''Brandon, can you hear me?''

He didn't answer, burrowing deeper until he no longer understood her words. Soon the syllables were as unreal as his pain; he registered only that the voice was full of colors, like opals. But even without words the sound was sad—the sound of things achingly lost and endlessly longed for.

He shifted on the cool sheets, and a knife of pain ripped into him. He stiffened, but he didn't try to escape it. He could bear the pain more easily than the sadness. If only she would go away and leave him alone.

But she didn't. Warm fingers wrapped around his wrist, and their touch wrenched him from the peaceful oblivion. He knew that touch. A memory began to form. Those fingers, that voice—

No! Sweat broke out on his brow, soaking the bandages that covered his eyes. His fingers twitched helplessly. He wanted to gather her into his arms and soothe her. And yet he must not. He curled his fingers into his palm. If he touched her, something would come of it so terrible it had no name.

Torn between the desire to remember and the need to forget, he felt the muscles all over his body twist. *Go,* he prayed, *before it's too late.* And then she lifted his hand to her lips, dropping a kiss and a tear on it. For a moment the darkness was ablaze, and he remembered everything.

Beauty. Passion.

Kelsey. Oh, my love, my love, what have we done?

Betrayal.

He groaned once as the light grew too bright to bear, and then it exploded, shattering the memory into a thousand pieces, pieces so small and jagged they could never be put together again.

CHAPTER TWO

THE SKY ABOVE CLIFF ROAD was as innocently blue as if it had never seen a cloud, much less a storm. Still, as Kelsey passed the spot where Brandon had lost control of his car, she couldn't help clenching her bandaged hands in her lap.

"You okay?" The man in the driver's seat sounded anxious, and she managed a brief, reassuring smile. Greg Siddons was a nice guy, but he was barely twenty, and his two months of service as Kelsey's secretary clearly hadn't prepared him for a role in this Traherne melodrama. Until today, when he'd been assigned to pick her up at the hospital, he hadn't been required to do anything more dramatic than cancel lunch reservations.

"I'm fine," she said, relaxing her hands as the rental car swept past the scene, which had been stripped of all signs of the accident. No twisted metal, no dismembered trees, not even the glint of overlooked bits of glass. Only the instinctive acceleration of her heartbeat told her where she was.

Greg didn't look convinced, his brow knitted above his round glasses. Poor guy. Just out of business school, proud of his ninety words a minute, eager to please. But today she had reason to be very grateful for young Greg Siddons. She was going to need a secretary. With Douglas gone, she was the only one left who knew enough about Office Design of California, or ODC, as the Traherne family business was called, to keep it going.

And she was determined to do exactly that. When Brandon came home.... She tried to shut out the soft, deadly whisper that insinuated itself into her thoughts. *If* Brandon came home, it said. If, if, if... She took a deep breath. *When* Brandon came home, he would find things in order, prosperous and secure.

"How's Brandon doing?" Greg's voice broke in abruptly. "What do the doctors say?"

"They're optimistic." But her words had a hollow sound. She tried not to think of how Brandon had looked—so helpless, damaged, remote. Her first sight of him had taken her breath away, a tangle of tubes and wires. Blinking machines surrounded him, threatening in spite of their sterile indifference.

Worst of all, somehow, were the white bandages that wound thickly around his head, covering his eyes. Dr. James had told her they wouldn't know for a couple of weeks whether his vision had survived the accident.

Though she'd always loved them, until she couldn't see them, she hadn't fully appreciated how beautiful Brandon's eyes really were. Forest eyes—alternately green and brown, and shot through with golden sunlight. Rimmed with thick brown lashes and crowned with a strong, straight brow.

But those eyes had more than merely the blessing of physical beauty. The sunlight of his personality shone through them, too. Anyone looking into Brandon Traherne's eyes felt befriended and understood.

Standing by his bed, she had looked at the bruised mouth, battered out of its normal shape, its naturally uptilted corners dragged down by lacerations and swelling. And she had realized that, if she had to, she could live without Brandon's dazzling smile. But if she could never look into his eyes again... If she could never be warmed to laughter by their irresistible sparkle, never take ease from their gentle tolerance...

They were almost there. As they passed through the gates, the house came into sight, crouching on the crest of the hill, the three-story tower that bulged out of the north wing giving it a curiously deformed look. Kelsey suppressed a shiver. She did so hate this house!

Douglas had brought her to his small hometown about an hour outside of San Francisco when their engagement was announced two months ago. He wanted their wedding to be held at home, he'd said, and besides, ODC was courting an important client who lived nearby. Kelsey, who was in charge of the account, would be more useful if she was on hand at the Traherne mansion. Those were his official reasons, anyway. Kelsey had always suspected his real reason was the control it gave him over her. Sleeping under his roof, eating food from his table, miles from her father and her friends, with no transportation unless he lent her his car. Douglas had loved to control people.

The shiver broke through, and she studiously focused her mind on business. The important client had been real enough. Mr. Farnham. And Kelsey was still in charge of the negotiations. "Mr. Farnham didn't cancel, did he, when he heard about the accident?"

"No." Greg seemed relieved to change the subject, too. "He said he'd been dealing with you all along, not with Mr. Traherne, and he didn't want to wait. Kind of a fussy old codger, isn't he? But he seems to have a soft spot for you."

She smiled as he brought the car to a stop on the gravel driveway. "Calling the clients 'codgers' isn't a good idea," she warned him. "Especially a client who has thirty offices nationwide that he wants us to redesign."

Greg looked chastised, pushing his glasses nervously higher on his nose, and Kelsey shook her head, resisting the urge to pat his arm maternally. Though she was only twenty-six, she felt mature enough to be his mother. Maybe that came from having had to protect her own foolish father from the time her mother had died, when she was ten. She'd had to grow up early.

The urge to pat him faded, and Kelsey glanced instinctively down at her left hand. A flesh-colored bandage wrapped around the base of her third finger, where the windshield had sliced through the skin deeply enough to require four stitches. No one had commented on the absence of her engagement ring, a four-carat diamond that might have protected her finger.

If she'd been wearing it.

She curled her hand around the door handle tightly.

"Well, aren't we going to go in?" Greg was cleaning his glasses on his sleeve, and his voice was unnaturally high.

His face was turned carefully away from her as if he studied the house, though he was far too myopic to see anything from here. Kelsey wondered what he'd heard. A salacious mixture of truth and rumor, probably. It must make a great tale for the gossips—blood and amnesia, fire and rain, discarded diamonds and death.

But as wild as the gossips might make it, Kelsey doubted whether any of the tales were quite as wild as the truth.

"All right," she said, and she heard the dullness in her voice, the tired resignation. She drew a deep breath for courage and pushed open the door. "Let's go in."

SHE SLEPT FOR HOURS, and awakened to find her room plunged into a twilight gloom. It must be close to dinnertime. She forced herself to get up. She couldn't sleep forever, and reality, diabolically patient, would be there waiting for her. Might as well meet it with at least a show of bravado.

But as she stood beneath the shower, her thoughts again turned to Brandon. Maybe it was the feel of her wet hair against her shoulder blades or the warm spray of water against her cheeks, that brought back the memory of that crazy sailboat race across the bay....

Her life had changed that afternoon. It had been a balmy summer Sunday at the park, ODC's annual company picnic, an event Douglas had sponsored out of a sense of duty but never bothered to attend. Ginny, seeing in Brandon and Kelsey her first chance to attend the enticing party, had begged to go this year, and they had, with Douglas's blessing, agreed to take her.

Laden with Frances's fried chicken and sandwiches, the three of them had set off together. And it had been a wonderful day, as days away from Douglas usually were. Kelsey had laughingly declined to enter the three-legged race, but had cheered Brandon and Ginny across the finish line.

Somehow, though, they had talked her into entering the sailfish race. Tiny multicolored boats bobbed invitingly along the shoreline of the windy bay, and Brandon had assured her they were simple to sail. Giving in, Kelsey had peeled off her shorts and shirt down to her swimsuit. Just in case, she said, laughing, sailing wasn't as easy as he claimed.

It wasn't. The sun was high and hot, baking her arms and back, but the breeze was deceptively strong. Halfway across the bay she was amazingly in the lead, only a wave or two ahead of Brandon. But then a wayward gust of wind puffed her sail out like a balloon, and the boat tipped suddenly, seeming to stand on its side in the water.

Kelsey tried to hold on, but it was no use. She slid into the cold bay, and the boat toppled after her, the sail settling like a floating blanket over her head. Ducking under again, she edged around the sail and had just sputtered to the surface, a self-deprecating laugh ready on her lips, when she saw Brandon dive from his own boat.

He swam toward her with an urgent efficiency, covering the short distance in a flash. "Kelsey!" He joined her beside the capsized hull. "Are you okay?"

She nodded, tilting her head to shake water from her ears. "Just a little embarrassed."

To her surprise, he didn't return her smile. Rainbows flashed in the drops of water that had caught on his lashes, but underneath them, his eyes were deep and dark, filled with an intense concern.

"I was afraid," he said. "I thought it had hit your head." And then, slowly, gingerly, like a thief inching his way through unseen dangers to steal a forbidden prize, he reached out to touch her forehead.

She could still picture that moment. His hand, with rivulets of clear water threading its strong fingers, moving toward her in slow motion, hovering a fraction of an inch from her skin, then brushing her wet hair out of her eyes, probing silently for any sign of a bump or a bruise.

It was a confusing sensation, and Kelsey held herself very still. The water seemed to be inspecting her, too. It undulated inquisitively around her, lifting to cup her chin, then subsiding in a slow retreat to settle like a liquid collar around her neck. Farther down, an unseen current sucked at her, pulling her ever so slightly toward Brandon. Her fingers slipped on the boat's glossy fiberglass hull, and the foot of water that separated them narrowed to six inches.

And still his hand explored her face. Across her forehead, over her temple, behind her ear.

When his hand was buried up to the wrist in the dark, tangled wetness of her hair, he seemed to freeze, and his breath came out like a sigh. "Kelsey," he whispered, so softly she couldn't be sure it wasn't the wind in her ears. But then their eyes met, and she saw an expression in his that seemed to turn her bones into something as liquid as the bay itself. Again her grip faltered on the boat, and before she could steady herself his hand pressed against the back of her head, slowly, deliberately, guiding her toward him.

She didn't protest. Cold currents slipped past her, tingling against her thighs, sliding across her breasts. She shivered, and her hardened nipples strained against the swimsuit that molded her like a second skin.

When she was next to him, he let his hand drop, under the cloak of water, down along her bare back, down to where the fabric of her suit traced the curve of her bottom. His hand had the tender wonder of a lover's touch, and they were so close the water was warm from their combined heat.

He would have pulled her all the way, bringing them skin to skin, but she put her hand up between them, against the muscled wall of his chest. It should have been a gesture of firm refusal, but her palm fit so perfectly over the smooth mound of his pectoral muscle that her fingers relaxed. The touch became a caress so intimate that she could feel both the hard thrust of his nipple and the racing throb of his heart.

He parted his lips to speak—or to kiss—but he did neither, as if afraid to break the spell. She waited, caught in the liquid shivering, realizing numbly, as if watching from some disembodied height, that none of this could be seen by the others. Their bodies were invisible beneath the water, and this strange, subtle awakening was being born in complete secrecy.

Secrecy. The word, with all its dirty implications, finally brought her to her senses, and she was suddenly ashamed of his hand on her hip, of his heart beneath her palm. This wasn't some glorious mystery; it was just a sneaking grope between two people who had no right to touch each other except in the most superficial of ways.

With a desperate jerk she pulled free, and to her relief, he didn't try to stop her.

"We'd better get this boat upright before it sinks," she said brightly, hoping he'd join her in the pretense that nothing had happened.

And, thankfully, after a long moment of silence, when all she heard were little lapping sounds as the bay licked at the overturned boat, he did. With practiced ease he pushed the exposed rudder back under the water, and the sailfish obediently rocked back into its normal position.

As if she were encased in an impenetrable armor of ice, Brandon did not touch her again for days. Miserable days when her palm tingled where his heart had been, when her body ached where his hands had been. Endless nights when she couldn't sleep, thinking of the currents that had pulled her into his arms. How long, she thought, had those unseen, dangerous currents been lying just below the surface?

No, he didn't touch her for days, not until the day of the accident. And then only because he couldn't stop himself—

"Hello in there!"

With a start, Kelsey realized that Frances, the Trahernes' housekeeper, had been rapping on her outer door, announcing the arrival of her dinner tray. Taking a swift last look in the mirror, she hurried to open the door.

"Lord, child," the older woman said when she caught sight of Kelsey. "You look like something a drowned rat dragged in."

Kelsey couldn't help smiling. Frances had come to California from Germany fifty years ago, so in many ways she was as American as Kelsey herself. During the weeks Kelsey had lived at the Traherne house, though, she had observed that Frances occasionally chose to ease tense moments by affecting a comical foreign confusion.

And there had been plenty of tense moments.

She took the tray from the housekeeper with a grateful smile. It smelled delicious, warm and aromatic, fresh from the kitchen. "Is Ginny home yet? She was playing over at Marcy Atwood's house when I got back. I didn't mean to sleep so long—I wanted to talk to her."

"She's in her room," Frances said as she moved toward the bed to plump the pillows. "I took her tray in, but she's worried sick about her brother, and I don't think she's going to eat, poor little thing."

Kelsey's heart tightened, constricted by yet another twist to the vise of guilt that gripped her. Brandon's sister, Ginny, who was only twelve, had been her special ally in this house. And yet, that awful night, Kelsey had left without even saying goodbye.

"Did she ask to see me?"

The housekeeper shook her head. "No." The woman's eyes were sympathetic. "She's pretty shook up. She didn't want to talk to anybody."

Straightening one last wrinkle in the bedclothes, the older woman sighed. "It's the worry about Mr. Brandon that's getting to her. Mr. Douglas's death, well, that was hard news, of course. But Mr. Traherne was too old to be much of a brother to her. And he was always busy with the company. It's Mr. Brandon she misses. It was Mr. Brandon who made her laugh."

Kelsey blinked away sudden, stupid tears. "I know, Frances," she said, gripping her tray in hands stiff with tension. "Did you know he was teaching her to play football?"

Such a silly thing to remember now. But she'd never forget the afternoon—was it really only a week ago?—when she had stood at the picture window in Douglas's office, looking down at the manicured lawn, where Brandon and Ginny were running, tackling, tumbling, giggling. Caught in the pink glow of sunset, the picture had held a magical innocence, the purity of simple, devoted affection. As if she stared at a forbidden Eden, Kelsey hadn't been able to take her eyes away.

Douglas had noticed, of course. Smiling, he had insinuated one possessive hand into her hair, forcing her head toward his shoulder. As they stood there in that mockery of intimacy, he had slowly, sadistically, drawn the draperies closed.

God, she had hated him!

And his funeral was tomorrow.

Suddenly the smell of the meat on her plate filled her with nausea. Perspiration formed on her forehead and upper lip, and her fork rattled warningly against her plate.

"I think I'll go eat with Ginny," she said impulsively. She didn't think she could stand to be alone. She needed to be with someone who loved Brandon, too, even if that someone was a little girl who was sullen, nursing her pain and resentment.

Ginny didn't respond to her knock, so, balancing the tray on her knee, Kelsey opened the door without permission. At first she thought the girl wasn't even in the room, but as her eyes adjusted to the gloom, she saw her, huddled on the window seat.

"I didn't say come in." The young voice was heartbreakingly emotionless. Little girls shouldn't sound that way. They could sound pouty or furious, but not like this, not dead and flat.

"Sorry. I thought you must not have heard me." Cloaking her concern with a matter-of-fact air, Kelsey nudged the light switch with her elbow. The overhead fixture sprang to life, pouring dazzling yellow light into the room.

Ginny, who must have been sitting in the dark a very long time, blinked painfully. "Ow!" she complained, shielding her eyes. "I wanted it dark."

"But if it's dark you can't see your food."

Ginny squinted over at the untouched tray. "So what? I'm not eating, anyway."

"Well, I am." Kelsey sat down in the nearest armchair and picked up her fork. She ate silently, ignoring the black glares Ginny shot her way. Ginny's small body emanated tension; she sat as still as a statue.

"This is good." The succulent lamb was sticking in Kelsey's throat, but she didn't dare let Ginny guess that. "Try yours."

"I don't *want* it!" Ginny's voice rose.

"It's good, though," Kelsey insisted calmly, without looking up. She heard real emotion breaking through Ginny's apathy, and that was encouraging. Maybe she could reach her, after all.

"I said I don't *want* it!" Ginny jammed the heels of her hands into the window seat. She was close to tears now. Kelsey heard them just under the defiant words. "I didn't ask you to come in here to eat with me. Why did you come in here?"

The little voice cracked, and through the fissure came the tears. They rolled unchecked down her pale cheeks as she pressed her fists to her chest. "Why did you come back here at all? I never asked you to. I don't need you."

Swiftly Kelsey set down her tray and joined Ginny on the window seat. Taking the still-weeping girl into her arms, she held her, making soothing noises.

"Honey, it's okay." She rested her cheek against Ginny's soft blond hair, hair that was so much like Brandon's. "I know you're worried about him. But he's strong, you know. Just think how tough he is. He'll be fine."

For a while that was enough. In Kelsey's arms, Ginny's tight body relaxed. The storm of tears dwindled to a series of quiet hiccups and snuffles, and finally Ginny drew back, glaring at Kelsey with red-rimmed eyes.

"It's not just Brandon. It's— Why didn't you *tell* me you were leaving? I ran into your bedroom, and then I saw your little suitcase was gone and the picture of me you kept on your dresser, too." She squeezed Kelsey's arms, shaking them. "That's how I knew you were gone. It was awful," she said, choking on a sob. "Why were you going?"

For a moment no answer came. Though Kelsey had rehearsed this speech in the hospital, delicately phrasing and rephrasing to make the story suitable for a child's ears, in the face of Ginny's heartbroken accusation she couldn't even speak.

"I'm sorry," she said at last. "I shouldn't have left without telling you. You see, I decided I couldn't marry Douglas, and I told him so on the telephone." She took Ginny's hands in hers, letting their warmth soak into her cold fingers. "But your brother was very angry, and he was coming back here to talk to me about it. I wanted to leave before he got here. So Brandon said he'd drive me back to San Francisco."

Ginny tilted her head, a frown of curiosity furrowing her brow. "You mean you were running away from Douglas?"

Kelsey nodded. "I guess so. It wasn't very brave, was it?"

"Well..." Ginny's eyes had lost the accusing glare. "I know how you felt. It was hard to be brave around Douglas. He was kind of scary, especially when he was mad." One corner of her mouth twisted up in a wry smile. "I used to hide my report cards from him when I was little."

When she was little. Kelsey smiled, just a bit, and squeezed the girl's hands. "But I'm a grown-up," she pointed out. "I really ought to be braver."

"Oh, I don't know," Ginny said. "I've seen a lot of grown-ups who were afraid of Douglas. But if you thought he was scary, why were you going to marry him at all?"

Kelsey's mouth opened, but once again words failed her. Why, indeed? Ginny was too young to hear the answers, too young to know how often rotted wood lurked behind a pretty facade.

But she had to say something, even if it was a lie. "I—"

Just then the telephone rang, a sound straight from heaven. Giving Ginny an apologetic smile, Kelsey hurried to answer it.

It was Dr. James. "I wanted to let you know we've moved Brandon out of intensive care," he said, his voice unusually warm. "He's doing quite well. We're very encouraged."

Her knees weakening, Kelsey leaned against the table for support. A sound from heaven indeed. Shutting her eyes against the sting of tears, she gave a prayer of thanks.

"Miss Whittaker? Did you hear me?"

"Yes," she managed, though her voice sounded like a stranger's. "Yes, I heard you."

"Good. He's in room 411. We'll keep you posted."

She opened her eyes. "Doctor, wait! May I speak to him?"

A palpable silence, followed by the muffled sound of conversation, too low for her to catch the words. And then Dr. James was back, the warmth gone, replaced by his usual brisk authority.

"Miss Whittaker, I'm in Brandon's room right now. He wants to know if his sister is there. He'd like to speak to her."

A shaft of pain shot through her. He wanted to speak to Ginny. The rejection was clear and cruel. He would not talk to Kelsey.

For Ginny's sake, she fought the pain. She mustn't mind. Ginny was his sister. Ginny needed him, needed the reassurance of talking to the one brother she had left. But, oh, Kelsey needed him, too! Didn't he know that?

"Miss Whittaker?" Dr. James sounded impatient.

She held out the telephone. "Ginny," she said, her voice unrecognizable. "It's Brandon, honey. He's going to be all right."

CHAPTER THREE

SOMETIME DURING THE NIGHT it rained. Though the sun struggled out by morning, the earth smelled wet and was spongy underfoot as the funeral party climbed to the Traherne mausoleum.

Off to the left, the wind had tossed a wreath of yellow roses on its side, the legs of its metal stand sticking helplessly up into the air. Someone should right it, Kelsey thought as they passed. It looked startled lying so, and its vivid petals were matted with mud.

Exposed. Sullied. Like the Traherne family itself today.

On that thought, Kelsey shivered. It was blustery and cold, in spite of the sun's efforts. At first she had been surprised by how many people had braved the ugly weather to come to the cemetery to say goodbye to a man she knew they hadn't liked. But soon their furtive, sidelong glances and sibilant whispers had provided the explanation. It wasn't just a funeral. It was, at best, a business obligation; at worst, a sideshow.

"It's true," one whisperer insisted. "She wasn't in his car. She was in *Brandon's* car."

Stumbling on the sodden grass, Kelsey steadied herself on the wing of a angel that drooped in exhausted grief over a nearby tombstone. The marble was cold and slippery with algae. Kelsey pulled her fingers back, hid their green-smudged tips in the pocket of her dress and kept walking, refusing to acknowledge the whispers.

Ginny, shepherded at the front of the crowd by a distant cousin, was the only person crying, and occasionally one of her low sobs would float back to Kelsey on the chill air. Kelsey knew everyone expected her, as the bereaved fiancée, to weep, too, but she couldn't oblige them. She was too cold, and if she possessed any tears, they were frozen inside her.

They finally stopped in the shadow of the mausoleum, where the smell of rain-soaked ground and decaying leaves was so strong Kelsey felt momentarily faint. She edged away from the group, out into the sunlight, where the wind swept the minister's words away, and she breathed the cleaner air deeply as the pallbearers set the casket on its stand.

The mausoleum was not particularly grand. It was almost like a doll's house, white and square, just like the other little marble houses that sat on the hillside. The only difference was that the door to this one was open.

"Not quite splendid enough for *his* taste, is it?"

The gruff voice spoke low in her ear, and Kelsey whirled, startled out of her numbness, to face the man who had so suddenly appeared at her side.

"Dad!" She took his arm, appalled. His beefy Irish face, leprechaun cheeks pinkened by the wind, looked out of place among the others. "What are you doing here?"

"Same thing everyone else is doing, I imagine." Tim Whittaker's mouth was twisted in a mirthless smile as he let his blue gaze wander the crowd. "Celebrating."

Kelsey squeezed his forearm warningly. "Hush, Dad. That's not true. And it's cruel."

"Almost as cruel as the bastard himself." Her father lowered his voice, but it was filled with something that sounded unpleasantly like triumph. Unwilling to argue in front of everyone, she turned to face the minister. For several moments her father stood quietly submissive, but out of the corners of her eyes she could see him watching the proceedings cynically.

When the minister began to wind up the eulogy with a flourish of praise for the dead man, Tim Whittaker snorted, a quiet but eloquent sound. "Now there's a tough job. Trying to find something godly to say about Douglas Traherne, who never did any man a kindness in his whole black life."

"*Dad!*" Kelsey's whisper was intense.

"Well, it's true." Her father was unrepentant. "I always knew he'd come to a bad end. I was just afraid he'd go too late to do us any good. I was glad to see fate lend a hand."

"*Enough!*" Kelsey was shocked and slightly sickened. She knew her father hated Douglas, but to say such things here...

She nudged him farther away from the others. The service was breaking up, and the mourners had begun to shift into small, whispering clusters. Putting her back to the crowd so that no one could read her face, she grabbed him by both arms.

"Dad, listen to yourself! Are you really so selfish that you can believe a man died just for your convenience? Ginny and Brandon have lost a brother. He was their *family*, Dad, whatever else he was. And they loved him, no matter what he had done." She stopped, having drawn the parallel to their own situation as clearly as she dared. "Our problems are ours to deal with. This service is for the Trahernes. Respect that, or go home."

Her voice was unforgiving and completely unlike her, and when her father flushed, obviously shocked and shamed, a wretched sense of guilt washed over her. She was overreacting. And why? She tried to be brutally honest with herself. Perhaps her father's words upset her because they struck a chord in her own heart. Perhaps she, too, was selfishly glad to have been set free, glad that she would never have to be Douglas Traherne's wife, glad that her father would never have to go to jail.

"I'm sorry, Dad. I didn't mean to be so hard."

"No. *I'm* sorry, love." Her father put his warm, meaty palm over her cold cheek. "It's just that I hated the thought of you married to him. I knew how you felt about him. And it was all my fault." His blue eyes filled with a wetness that glistened in the sunlight. "I'd been looking for a way out for you, and I just couldn't think of anything."

He looked so miserable, his wavy white hair tossed into a boyish disarray by the wind and his eyes full of melancholy, that Kelsey almost felt guilty for the critical words that raced unbidden through her. But not quite. He couldn't think of anything? What about simply facing up to what he had done? He could have let Douglas go to the police about the stolen company money, money that Tim Whittaker had gambled away on horses, greyhounds, ball games, cards—anything and everything. What kind of father let his daughter pay his debts for him?

A weak one. The concept wasn't new to her. She'd always known it.

"It's okay, Dad." Choking down tears of her own, she covered his hand with hers. "It'll be okay. Just don't talk that way, not here, please."

"Oh, Kelsey, love, I'm sorry to be such a useless old man." He gathered her into his arms, and she rested her head against his shoulder. But she didn't have any tears to shed—his words had been a plea for forgiveness, not an offer of support. She patted his back, a broad back for a man of his height, and strong. Was it wrong to wish it had been strong enough to carry his own burdens?

"Kelsey. Are you okay?" Ginny's small, tear-filled voice broke into her thoughts, and Kelsey pulled away from her father. Here was someone else who needed comforting, someone too little to carry the weight of this day's sorrows.

She looked down at the girl, hoping her smile was steady. "I'm okay," she said. "How about you?"

"I want to see Brandon." Ginny frowned and blinked hard, as if forcing tears away. Her hair had been pulled back into a tight French braid, not the most becoming style for her small, freckled face, and her black dress didn't quite fit. She looked very much like the orphan she was. "You said you'd take me today. Can we go now?"

"Soon. Let's go back to the house and serve sandwiches and coffee for an hour, and then we'll go to the hospital."

Kelsey accepted Ginny's grateful hug with a growing sense of guilty anticipation. It might be wrong, on the day of Douglas's funeral, to be eager to see Brandon, but she couldn't help it.

Already her heart was racing, and she lifted her face, trying to feel the sun through the wind. Maybe by now Brandon had remembered. Maybe he was waiting for her to come, with the same eagerness in his heart. Maybe, with enough time and enough of the passion they had glimpsed so briefly, they could put everything back together.

Wishful thinking? She hugged Ginny's warm, wiry body more tightly and headed down the hill. No. Just plain, old-fashioned hope. And she wouldn't give it up until she had to.

As ANOTHER WARM TRICKLE of beef broth ran down his chin, Brandon finally gave vent to the string of curses that had been accumulating inside him all morning. The sound was as primal as a caged lion's roar, and he didn't hold back one syllable of his frustration. He didn't know if the nurse was in the room, and he didn't give a damn. He was tired of feigning patience.

Throwing the spoon onto the tray, he dashed at the offending moisture with the heel of his hand. Beef broth and Jell-O! Couldn't the sadists at least have given him food that didn't wiggle or drip?

"I *did* offer to feed you, Mr. Traherne."

Blast it, the nurse was still here. He could feel her disapproval as she fussed with the mess he'd made, clanking cheap cutlery against plastic dishes and dabbing at his hospital robe with short, businesslike pokes.

"I'm not an infant," he said tersely. "If you'd give me real food, I'd manage just fine."

"If we gave you real food, you'd probably vomit. Much better to clean up a little broth, don't you think?"

Her voice had a suspicious innocence, as if she might be smiling. Brandon turned toward the sound, forgetting for one split second that his eyes were wrapped and taped and useless. Furious with himself for the lapse, he brought his head stonily back to the center and didn't answer.

"We're not in very good spirits today, are we?" When she grabbed his hand without warning, he had to fight the urge to wrench it away. Ignoring his twitch of resistance, she pressed his wrist between an astonishingly strong thumb and forefinger.

"It must be because you refused to take your medication." Her vague-sounding voice told him her mind was absorbed with counting his pulse, which he knew was beating much too fast, fueled by his impatience. "You'd feel a lot better if you'd take it."

He shook his head. Starting today, no matter how much his body complained, he was through with the medicine. He needed to be able to think properly, and he couldn't think at all in that zoned-out twilight of painkillers.

Besides, he could endure the pain. At least it assured him that, though he couldn't even see his own hands, he really was alive.

"I don't want the damn medicine."

He could tell she was rolling the tray away; the anemic meat smell of the broth was fading. Then, with disconcerting abruptness—damn those soft-soled nurse's shoes—she was at his side again, shoving up his shirtsleeve and wrapping the blood pressure cuff around his upper arm.

"Yes, so you've told me." She pumped until the cuff bit into his skin. "But your language! I'm beginning to long for the good old days, when you were in that nice, polite coma."

The chuckle in her voice was blatant now, and his lips curved into a smile in spite of himself.

"Too bad there's no way to send me back under, isn't it?"

"Well—" she let the air back into the cuff with a whoosh "—I've heard that a two-by-four, applied with surgical precision to the side of the head . . ."

At last he laughed. And despite the way it set off sparks of pain behind his eyes, the laughter felt good. More natural, somehow. More the way he used to be.

"That's more like it." Eerily echoing his thoughts, the nurse patted his arm and, gathering up the tray with another clatter of cutlery, left the room.

More like the way he used to be. He slumped against the pillows, the laughter dying. Would he ever really be like that again? When he got out of this damned hospital his whole life would be different.

For starters, what about his eyes? Dr. James had already warned him that his vision might be damaged permanently. No, not damaged. Destroyed. *Blind.* The very word panicked him, and his hands gripped the bandages at his temples as his eyes darted from right to left, finding only a claustrophobic blackness.

But all the injured places protested with silent flashes of pain, and he had to force himself to stop. Tension only made the pain worse. Sliding down until he lay flat on the mattress, he breathed deeply, consciously relaxing his muscles. Legs first, beginning with the broken toes, then focusing on the torn ligaments in his knee. Next the pelvis and lower back, where the sprained muscles had tied themselves into knots. Then arms and chest and neck.

It helped. The pain backed off a few paces, not vanquished but at least in wary retreat.

Yes, life would be different, but he could face whatever it would become. Douglas was dead. Which meant that he, Brandon, no longer had the luxury of being the happy-go-lucky brother, the archaeologist who wouldn't be cooped up in an office, the one who traipsed off to dig in wet, green jungles for forgotten treasures, who breezed back into town to tip the servants without having to sign any paychecks, to play games with Ginny without having to pick out her private school or take her to the doctor.

Now he had to be the president of ODC, the family business that needed protection because it would someday be Ginny's legacy. He had to be the head of the household, Ginny's guardian, the employer of five hundred people, the owner of stocks and bonds and real estate. He had inherited all that Douglas had left behind, the good and the bad.

And Kelsey?

Ignoring the pain, he squeezed his eyes, trying to force away the ridiculous thought. No one could *inherit* a fiancée, and he certainly wouldn't want to inherit Kelsey even if he could. He knew what kind of fiancée Kelsey had been.

During the month he'd been living at the cliff house, he'd noticed a lot. Too much. He'd seen the arctic chill Kelsey could give Douglas when he touched her. Once or twice he'd been in the guest bath, still wet from his shower and unable to escape, when Douglas had come knocking at Kelsey's door.

It had been sickening. His brother's voice had been thick with a hungry pleading, which soon gave way to angry insistence. Kelsey's refusals had been soft, too low for Brandon to make out anything except their tenor of implacable rejection.

Brandon could imagine how difficult that rejection must have been to accept. Kelsey Whittaker was a beautiful woman, her blue eyes wide and liquid with sensuality, her brown hair long and wanton, her body every man's dream. How could Douglas help wanting her? How could any man?

Those nights, while Douglas had begged for admittance to Kelsey's room, Brandon had felt a twisting in his own gut, a burgeoning of desire that made him bend weakly over the sink, supporting his weight on the heels of his hands and staring into his feverish eyes until the feeling finally passed.

And it did pass. He'd forced it to, that night and every other night. Except for his suspicions that she was just marrying Douglas for the Traherne money, Brandon had liked Kelsey Whittaker fine—she was smart and funny and seemed to have a good heart. Look at the way she always treated Ginny.

But the physical part had really been getting out of hand. It had reached the point that he couldn't even be in the same room as she was without going all cold and unsettled inside. And that day at the picnic—God, what a disgrace! It had been a real battle ever since he had felt her wet, wonderful body close to his and wanted more.

But he had won the battle, and God willing, she had never even known he was fighting it. He hadn't ever said anything, hadn't allowed himself even a little innocent flirtation, which had been his usual way of dealing with women. It wouldn't have been innocent with Kelsey, though, and he knew it was too dangerous. If his body crackled with electricity every time she came around, that had to be his guilty secret.

No, he hadn't allowed himself to covet his brother's fiancée, at least not openly. Thank God he'd controlled himself. He couldn't live with that, now that Douglas was dead.

But what the hell had really happened that night? He ran his hand roughly through his hair and leaned back against the pillow. How could he have forgotten? It was maddening and somehow embarrassing, and he felt furious and thwarted every time he tried to catch those elusive, mocking strands of memory.

Maybe he'd try one more time, think it through slowly, one step at a time. The last thing he remembered was at about six o'clock that night. He was playing football with Ginny—

"Brandon!" Lost in his grim thoughts, he didn't hear the door open. Only the delighted squeal and a soft rush of air announced Ginny's arrival. Brandon turned toward the sound just in time to receive the kisses she showered on his neck as she threw herself onto the bed.

Ignoring the pain that stabbed into his hand when her elbow pressed against the IV needle, he wrapped his free arm around her angular little body. She burrowed into his chest, innocently unaware of the sharp protest from his bruised ribs. "Hi, there, pesky." His voice thickened on the familiar teasing endearment, and he kissed the top of her head. "How's my girl?"

"Terrible." Now that she was safe in his embrace, Ginny's overly effusive greeting had changed, as he had suspected it would, to tears. "I've missed you so bad. I've been scared."

His grip tightened around her waist. "Don't be scared, sweetheart," he said, striving for a tone of easy confi-

dence. He had managed to calm her fears last night on the
telephone, but it would be more difficult today, when she
confronted his condition with her own eyes. "I told you.
Everything's going to be okay."

"No, it's not," she said stubbornly, sniffing. "What
about you? Are you going to be okay?"

Feeling with his untethered hand, he found her chin and
lifted it. It trembled pitifully, and a warm tear rolled onto his
thumb. "I'm going to be fine," he said, forcing his sore lips
into a smile. After only a short moment her trembling intensified, and she tried to duck her chin again. He held it up
firmly with the knuckle of his index finger. "Look at me,
Ginny. I know I look like somebody from a science-fiction
movie, but it's really not so bad. A few scrapes and bruises,
that's all."

"But you—" Ginny's indrawn breath was a sob. "Your
eyes."

"My eyes are going to be fine, too, as soon as they take
these mummy wraps off." Panic, which was becoming all
too familiar, gripped his gut even as he voiced the certainty.
Would he be fine? Or would he be blind forever? For Ginny's sake, he wrestled the fear into quick submission and
braced his smile. "You'll probably have to lead me around
by the hand for a while, though, to keep me from bumping
into furniture and stuff."

Her chin moved under his hand again, this time the skin
stretching up into what had to be a smile. "Yeah?" she said,
obviously intrigued. "Kind of like a seeing-eye dog?"

He grinned. "Kind of like a seeing-eye sister."

"Cool." She sounded self-satisfied. "I think I'd be good
at that. I'll have to be sure nobody moves any of the furniture around. I've seen that on TV. Blind people learn where
all the furniture is, and then if anybody moves it they get

really mad." She turned her head. "We'll tell Frances to be careful when she vacuums, won't we, Kelsey?"

Kelsey! Brandon's hand dropped like a stone, and his smile froze. He hadn't even suspected that Kelsey was in the room.

But she was. Her voice, strained and artificial, came from the other side of the bed. "Yes, honey, we'll tell her."

An unexpected anger coiled in Brandon's chest. She had been standing there the whole time, watching him... Although he hadn't minded having Ginny see him, he found the idea of Kelsey staring at him horrible. He knew how pathetic he must seem, how helpless with his stained hospital gown, his dripping IV tube, his useless eyes. He hated it. He had a stupid macho urge to rip the IV out of his hand, tear the bandages from his head and leap roaring to his feet, ordering her from the room.

Instead, he said, "Hello, Kelsey," in a tone that was frigid with repressed frustration. "I didn't realize you were here." The sharp antiseptic odor of the hospital must have cloaked the delicate scent of lilacs that always seemed to cling to her clothes. Sweet, sexy and uniquely Kelsey. It would have warned him.

Giggling, Ginny thumped his chest. "How did you think I got here, dummy? You think I hitchhiked?"

"I brought Ginny over right after the—" Kelsey seemed to stumble over the word "—after the funeral."

Her voice was muffled and strangely diffident. He wished fiercely that he could see her face. Was this merely a bit of theatrics, trying to demonstrate how grieved she was over her lost fiancé? He tightened his lips. No need for her to pull that act with him, not after he had heard those late-night scenes at her bedroom door.

"The service went very well, I think." The strain in her voice was growing, and he felt a cruel pleasure at the sound.

He didn't speak, though he knew that made her even clumsier. "The minister said..." She hesitated. "He said some lovely things. And the weather was cold, but clear. It rained last night, but it had stopped. And a lot of people came, a lot of people from the office..."

Her voice dwindled off, followed by small scraping sounds as she moved something nervously around on the nightstand.

In the awkward ensuing silence, Brandon's conscience was pricked slightly. It shouldn't have been this easy to disconcert Kelsey. She was a businesswoman and, judging from the little he'd seen the past month, a competent one. Why did she sound so vulnerable, as though she needed a supportive word from him?

She drew a jagged breath. "I'm so sorry about Douglas, Brandon," she said, the words tumbling out in a rush. "I'd wanted to tell you, but when I came you were sleeping." She put her hand on his arm, slipping her cold fingers under the IV.

She had been standing closer than he realized. The touch surprised him, and he twitched his arm. He controlled it well—it was merely a subtle flexing of muscle—but she must have noticed it. She whipped her hand away, as if his skin had burned the ice of her fingers. The IV pinched into the back of his hand as her hasty retreat jostled the tube.

"I'm sorry," she said again, awkwardly. "About Douglas. I know how much you and Ginny must be hurting."

She was good, he had to admit that. Sympathy dripped from her voice like the glucose that dripped from the IV. She had a beautiful voice—he realized it only now that he wasn't distracted by her face—or her body. A warm, persuasive voice. If he didn't know better, he might believe she really cared.

"And you, too, of course," he responded bitterly, angered as much by his own reluctant admiration as by her artificial concern. "I know exactly how much *you're* hurting right now."

If only for Ginny's sake, he hadn't meant the sarcasm to be quite that blatant, but he didn't seem to have much control over his voice or his emotions these days.

Kelsey pulled in a startled gasp of air. "Brandon, you know I . . . you know I feel—"

He didn't say a word, but as he turned his face toward her she stopped abruptly. Perhaps his disgusted disbelief was apparent in the squared set of his jaw, the tight line of his mouth. Was she really going to pretend that she grieved for Douglas?

He held his posture, rigid in this one-sided staring match, until he heard her deep, shaking exhalation. It was a defeated sound, and he knew she would never finish the sentence. Like a boxer returning to the safety of his corner, he lay his head against the pillow, curiously ashamed of himself. It had been, in a strange way, too easy. It was as if he fought a battle he had already won, against an opponent who wouldn't defend herself.

No. He flicked the thought away. Not wouldn't, *couldn't*. She couldn't defend herself. She knew she'd never loved Douglas. Well, now she knew that Brandon knew it, too.

A bustle of activity brought his head up. His hands balled involuntarily into fists. How infuriating it was to be blind! He couldn't tell where she was or what she was doing. He couldn't even look out the window and see if it was raining. Sunny or gloomy—it was all the same wretched nothingness to him.

"I think I'll go down and get a cup of coffee." When Kelsey finally broke the silence, her voice was surprisingly firm again. It was, in fact, nearly as icy as Brandon's had been. "I'll come get you in about half an hour, Ginny. Okay?"

Ginny must have nodded, because Brandon heard light, purposeful footsteps heading toward the door. "Okay, then. See you in a little bit."

And then, before he could answer her, she was gone. Which was what he wanted, wasn't it? But, perversely, instead of the vindicated relief he'd expected to feel, he was overcome by a sense of emptiness.

If he hadn't found the idea ridiculous, he would have said that the darkness in front of his eyes was blacker, more hopelessly impenetrable than ever.

CHAPTER FOUR

KELSEY RAN.

She ran until her thighs burned, and her muscles were as tight as iron. She ran past the quaint ice-cream parlors and art galleries of the town's one commercial street; past the park, where dogs and children romped in the soft grass; past other joggers who, not being driven by devils, kept a saner pace.

She ran until she could run no more, and then, giving up, she flung her aching, glistening body onto one of the benches that overlooked the water.

For a moment she simply stared unseeingly out at the cinema-perfect scene below her. Nestled between two hills that circled it in a protective embrace, the bay was mauve with reflected sunset. A light wind nudged the few remaining boats toward the marina in a slow parade of pink-tinted sails. High in the hills, the lights began to wink on in front porches and in kitchen windows. Night was falling, and the entire world seemed at peace. Everyone, that was, except Kelsey.

Her breath came more evenly now, but her mind was still in turmoil. She hadn't been able to outrun her confusion, after all. She kneaded a bunched-up muscle in her thigh with the ball of her thumb and tried to decide what she should do.

Brandon was coming home tomorrow.

On an emotional seesaw, she rode first elation and then despair at the thought. Brandon was coming home, but what did that mean for her?

It had been a week since she had seen him. After that first fiasco, she hadn't tried to visit him again, unable to bear the knowledge that she was little more than an unwelcome stranger. She had waited in the lobby for Ginny or stayed at home, tending the business and running the household. But every morning she awoke with new hope. Maybe this would be the day he would remember.

Surely such potent memories couldn't just disappear like a formless, odorless gas. But apparently, for Brandon, they had. He hadn't called, except to talk to Ginny. He hadn't once asked to see Kelsey.

Obviously her hopes for a poignant reunion had been preposterously naive. Obviously she had read far, far too much into their one night of passion. Rather than spin pretty kaleidoscope dreams about that night, she'd be much wiser to do what Brandon already had done: forget it had ever happened.

Yes, she must forget. And she would. Soon.

But not yet. She shut her eyes, her thumb rubbing rhythmically over the painful muscle in her leg, and allowed herself to remember it all one last time.

Ironic, really, that her whole world had been changed because of a silly football game.

It had seemed like such innocent fun—just Kelsey and Ginny and two of Ginny's young friends horsing around in the late summer sun. Kelsey should have been working, but Douglas was in San Francisco overnight, and with him gone she felt deliciously free and lighthearted. And she was getting pretty good at catching Ginny's passes. In fact, she had just landed flat on her nose at the edge of her imaginary goalpost, having been brought down by Marcy Atwood's flying tackle, when Brandon showed up.

"Touchdown!" she hollered, scrambling ungracefully to her knees and holding the football triumphantly aloft.

Ginny whooped. "That's twenty-one zip," she called out. "Sounds like you guys are history!"

"Sounds to me like the teams are lopsided," Brandon suggested dryly from the sidelines, which had been delineated with a straggling trail of cypress mulch and pebbles. "Maybe Marcy and Tom need a grown-up on their team, too."

No one had realized he was there, and for a minute four pairs of eyes stared at him in surprise. He was smiling with that half-cocked, teasing grin that Kelsey found so heart-meltingly attractive, and his sweatshirt was the same corn-field gold as his hair. Even twelve-year-old Marcy Atwood was gazing at him with innocent admiration. Tom, Marcy's fourteen-year-old brother, just looked glad to have another male around.

Then Ginny squealed, her bumptious air forgotten in her pleasure, and she threw herself at her brother. "All *right!*" she cried. "Will you really play with us, Brandon?"

"In the interest of justice, I think I have to," he said with mock solemnity, tugging on what was left of his sister's braid. Kelsey felt a warm rush of pleasure. What a wonderful day it was turning out to be! And there were many hours of freedom left. Douglas wouldn't be home until noon tomorrow.

Laughing and whispering, they divvied up into teams, and over the next twenty minutes, as the sun began its slow retreat over the bay and rain clouds gathered on the horizon, the gap in the score tightened.

Concerned about the darkening sky, Kelsey warned the kids that they had time for only one last play. Ginny motioned Kelsey to run deep for a long pass, but as soon as she caught it, Kelsey felt Brandon just behind her, lunging forward, as she hurtled toward the end zone, the area where the grass gave way to a garden bed of three-foot-high snapdragons.

He was so close she could hear his breath, coming hard as he fought to strip the ball from her. But she clutched the ball to her chest and, neither one willing to relinquish their hold, they tumbled heavily into the flowers together.

Thick stems cracked under their weight, and yellow-throated snapdragons fell to their deaths all around them, but Kelsey barely noticed the destruction. Even the precious football, which had been jarred loose on impact, drifted to a stop somewhere beside her and was forgotten.

None of that mattered, not anymore. She knew only that Brandon lay on top of her, his face buried in a pillow of flowers, his labored breath warm against her neck. How long did they lie that way, hidden from the others by the tall stalks of snapdragons? It could have been a second or a century. Time slowed to a crawl, and she was mesmerized by every rise and fall of his hard-muscled chest against her softer contours. Every subtle movement of his body was intensified, and though she could barely breathe, she had never felt more alive, more aware.

Because she was so intensely focused on every inch of him, she knew the instant awareness hit him. At first it was just a frisson of tension that shuddered through him, right below the surface. Then his breath snagged, skipping a beat before resuming its heavy rhythm. Then, slowly, he lifted himself onto his elbows—the motion thrusting even more of his weight onto his hips, until his face hovered just inches over hers. And there, in that private world of soft flowers and timelessness, his eyes met hers in a moment of unguarded truth.

Oh, his eyes! She had always thought of them as forest eyes, sometimes cool and deep, sometimes sparkling with sunlight, always filled with an extraordinary sensuality. But this was different. The beautiful forest had somehow caught fire, and everything was ablaze, with a scorching, devouring heat.

Groaning slightly, as if the fire were a pain inside him, he shifted, his thighs settling on either side of her legs, which suddenly felt liquid and boneless. Right there, at the point at which they were hinged, another fire was building, and though she could tell by the rigidity of his torso that he fought it desperately, his body burgeoned as desire swept through him.

He didn't pull away, didn't try to hide what he was feeling, but as a low gasp escaped her parted lips, he groaned again and leaned his head back in a gesture of bewildered regret.

"Kelsey, I'm sorry..." But the fire was rapacious, and it was out of his control. The blatant evidence of his need exposed him, and lowering his head, he met her gaze with eyes that held a question.

An intense warmth rushed through her blood—her body's primitive, unequivocal answer to that question. She reached up with shaking fingers to touch his face.

"I know," she whispered. "It's all right."

"No." He shut his eyes against her touch. He held himself in an unnatural rigidity for one last second, and then, finally, slowly, as if he fought against quicksand, he pulled away, rolling onto the ground beside her.

Suddenly time resumed its normal pace, and she heard the laughing voices of Ginny and her friends approaching. The whole searing episode had taken only a few stolen seconds.

"No," he said again, in a bleak voice. He stood and held out his hand to help her. "It's not all right. It's all wrong."

There was no time to contradict him, no time to tell him that, in her own, less conspicuous way, she had felt the same confused and uncontrollable desire. The children were running up, both amused and horrified that the adults had been the ones to destroy the precious flower beds.

"Ooh, Brandon!" Ginny's teasing voice broke through, and they turned toward her, where she stood on the edge of the flower bed, waving a sadly mistreated snapdragon smugly. "Look what you did! Douglas is going to kill you!"

Instinctively Kelsey's gaze shot to Brandon's face. Had he caught the darker implications of Ginny's innocent threat? He had. His teeth were clenched so hard his jaw looked absolutely square and a muscle jumped violently in his cheek.

But he didn't look at her. He rose to his feet, brushing mulch from his sleeves and saying something back to his sassy sister. Kelsey rose, too, and stood behind the others, feeling a little dizzy, and tried to calm her racing thoughts.

She didn't know exactly what was happening, but she did know one thing. She could never, no matter what happened, marry Douglas Traherne now.

Somehow she reached her room and, controlling the urge to throw herself onto the bed and weep into the pillow, she sat rigidly in the armchair, arms crossed over her chest, and tried frantically to think.

For the past month she had struggled against her growing fondness for Brandon, pretending that this unthinkable thing wasn't happening. She *couldn't* be falling in love.

But she was. Love. Unwise, unplanned, heartbreaking love. Deep inside, she had known it for weeks. When he passed her a glass, her fingers tingled. When she brushed against him in the hall, her body trembled. When he laughed, her heart was merry. When he wasn't around, her soul felt bereft. And when she slept, she dreamed of him.

Her insides twisted, and she grabbed a pillow and squeezed it to her chest. Love. For her fiancé's brother. Where in the name of all that was decent did that leave her?

For a blessed minute out there in the garden the answer had seemed so clear. Brandon's words were true: It was all wrong. All wrong to marry a man she detested. All wrong to let Douglas get away with such hideous blackmail. All wrong to encourage her father to dodge the consequences of his actions.

A voice inside her began to raise the inevitable doubts. Wasn't she rationalizing, trying to free herself at her father's expense? Would she really send her father to jail so that she could sleep with Brandon Traherne? What kind of selfish daughter would do such a thing?

She pounded the pillow in frustration. Was there no ethical high ground she could ever attain in this grueling mental debate? It seemed there was no right and wrong here. Only wrong and wrong.

Unable to sit quietly any longer, she paced the room like a caged animal, opening drawers pointlessly, rearranging cosmetics and restacking books. But nothing she did brought her any closer to an answer—not until she flung open the door to the closet.

Like a ghost swooping toward her, a flash of white swirled in the rush of air. Shocked, she backed away, and then, as she identified the soft white material, she had to stifle a cry. Sometime during the day someone had delivered her wedding dress.

She hadn't known the dress was ready yet. She had bought it only a few weeks ago, but the seamstress had already needed to alter it, tucking in seams to make up for the weight Kelsey had lost since she'd been living in Douglas's house.

It was a gorgeous dress. Made entirely of lace and satin; seed pearls running in a trickle of moonglow down the back; calf-length with a full, flowing skirt.

And yet the sight of it filled Kelsey with so much revulsion she was afraid she might be physically sick.

She tried to imagine Douglas lying above her, as Brandon had done today, his body on fire with the desire to possess her, a desire she had managed to turn aside so far—but a desire that he could indulge to his heart's content once they were married.

Her stomach tightened, forcing a bilious acid up toward her throat. Oh, God... And, with that image, the sickness overcame her. Slamming the door shut, as if she could trap the thoughts in the closet with the horrible dress, she rushed to the bathroom, and there was dreadfully, shamefully ill.

When the nausea passed, it left her trembling and weak, but finally sure that nothing could make her go through with this marriage. She slid off her ring and, slipping it back into its velvet box, walked quickly to Douglas's office to shove it into one of the drawers in his desk.

Feeling nervous and guilty, like a prisoner plotting an escape, she hurried back to her own quarters. Then, as if to scrub away all trace of Douglas's ownership, she took a hot, hard shower. Afterward, skin pink and tingling, she wrapped her blue silk robe around herself and returned to her bedroom. Shutting her door behind her, she leaned against it and stared at the telephone, which suddenly seemed like a dangerous weapon. Nonsense, she scolded herself. Just do it. Call him and get it over with.

Her fingers shook as she tried to pick up the telephone, and she dropped the receiver back into its cradle with a nervous clatter. Her pulse was beating so fast in her throat she wondered whether she would be able to speak at all.

For a moment she thought about venturing downstairs to the liquor cabinet, where Douglas kept bottles of over-priced alcohol to impress his clients and friends. But suppose she encountered Brandon? No, she couldn't risk it.

But wait—she had a bottle of wine here in her room. Given to them by one of the secretaries when their engagement had been announced, it wasn't expensive enough to rate the downstairs cabinet, so Douglas had told her to keep it.

It tasted terrible, but it was worth it. After the first few swallows, she felt steadier.

A dank darkness was gathering prematurely outside her window, as the rain clouds continued their slow roll inland. Thunder rumbled somewhere in the distance, an ominous sound, like an angry voice raised behind the closed doors of a far-off room. There would be a storm before the night was out.

She ought to turn on a light. Everything, including the wine she poured into her rapidly softening paper cup, was cast in sickly gray shadow. But she didn't. She sat on the edge of the bed, staring at the phone, and drank her wine like medicine.

By the fourth cup she decided she was ready, and she began to dial.

"Douglas." She launched right in, not wanting to give herself time to think. "I have something to tell you."

"Is it Farnham?" He sounded irritable. He probably had an important client waiting. He'd resent being delayed.

But actually, he always sounded irritable when he talked to her. Always. Unless, of course, someone was listening, or it was late at night and he'd had a few drinks and was feeling sexy. Then he was as syrupy as a man could be.

Sickness pushed again at the back of her throat, and she tried to shove the thoughts away.

"No, it's not about Mr. Farnham," she said, annoyed to hear herself slur the words. She didn't want him to think she was saying these things because she was drunk. "It's about us."

"Oh?" Doubt crept into his voice. "What about us?"

"I'm not going to do it, Douglas. I'm not going to marry you." The sentences came out in a breathless rush. But at least they were out. She turned her face to the open window, and a gust of mercifully cool air blew over her.

"What are you talking about?" His voice was bullying, as if he thought he could control her with his tone alone.

"I'm not going to marry you," she repeated, enunciating each word carefully. "The wedding is off. The engagement is off." She inhaled deeply. "The deal is off."

"Oh, really?" Suddenly he sounded smug, as if the word "deal" had reminded him he still had the ace of spades up his sleeve. "You've decided to let your father go to jail?"

"Not exactly." She had thought all this through. Now if only her head would stay clear enough for her to explain herself to Douglas. "My father needs professional help. Doctors, lawyers—people who can do more than just cover up his problems. People who might even be able to help him get well." She tried to believe her own brave words. "Maybe he'll have to go to jail. I don't know. I guess we'll see."

"*Maybe?*" Douglas laughed, a bone-chilling sound. "*Maybe* he'll have to go to jail? Listen to me, sweetheart. If you back out now, I guarantee you your father will rot in jail."

"Maybe," she repeated stubbornly.

"Damn it, Kelsey, are you drunk? You sound drunk. Or are you just crazy?" Outside, the thunder growled like a stalking beast that grew more daring as it closed in on its prey.

"Listen to me." Douglas's voice had the same threatening quality. "You sit right where you are. I'm coming home. I'll be there in two hours, and then I've got something to show you."

"No," she said mulishly. "I don't want to see anything."

"You'll want to see this. It's an IOU your father signed. He's a thief, and he's going to jail. I should have shown the damn thing to you right away. Maybe then you wouldn't have gotten this stupid notion in your head."

"No," she repeated stubbornly as a brilliant flash of lightning blinked through the room. "I don't want to see it."

"Well, you're going to. You just stay right there. And don't drink any more. When I get home, I'm going to explain the facts of life to you, sweetheart—"

But she was shivering, her head was reeling, and she couldn't listen to him. "Goodbye, Douglas," she said, and with fingers that shook like jelly, she hung up.

"Goodbye," she whispered. Then, before a reaction could settle in, she picked up the phone again and dialed her father's number. She had to warn him. They had so much to do and so little time. They had to hire a lawyer....

But the telephone in their little apartment rang and rang emptily. She squeezed the receiver. What racetrack, which bar, had lured him away tonight, when she needed him most?

And then, suddenly, she began to cry. Silent tears rolled down her cheeks, down her neck, until the front of her robe was wet. And still she sat, the receiver in her lap, listening to the ever-closer thunder and the tragic sound of endless ringing.

She barely heard the knock at her door. Even when the door opened slowly, she didn't look up.

"Kelsey?"

Finally she turned her head. It was Brandon, silhouetted in the doorway. Though she could hardly see him, she knew he had showered, too. He smelled fresh and clean. The scent carried across the shadows, and stupidly, she began to cry anew.

"Kelsey, what's the matter?"

He shut the door behind him, crossed the room rapidly, and knelt on the floor beside her.

"What's wrong?" He saw the telephone in her lap and picked it up. Holding it to his ear, he frowned quizzically, then cradled the receiver on its base. "Who were you calling?"

"My father," she said brokenly, wiping at her damp chin, then her cheeks, ashamed of her tears. "He's not home."

His frown tightened as he noticed the wine bottle beside the telephone, but he didn't comment on it. Instead, he reached up and brushed the tears from her face.

"Well, that's not so terrible, is it? He'll be back soon."

"But I need him now," she said, her eyes on her hands, which lay helplessly in her lap. "I need him to take me home."

Her voice had risen, but she couldn't seem to help it. The wine's bracing effects had evaporated, leaving behind a swampy mess of ungovernable emotion. Still, she tried not to cry. She didn't want him to think she was hysterical.

She reached instinctively for the cup of wine, wanting to return to the insensate peace it had offered her before. But in one swift movement Brandon's hand caught hers and held it back.

"Kelsey, honey," he said. "You don't need that."

Finally she gathered the courage to look at him, and the expression she saw in his eyes told her she needn't have worried. This was *Brandon,* not Douglas, who would have ordered her to shape up and grow up. Not her father, who was so needy himself that he couldn't tolerate any sign of weakness in her.

No, miraculously, this was Brandon, whose sympathies were quick and warm, whose strength was like a bottomless cup from which she was invited to sip, whose eyes were filled with understanding, even when he looked at the wine bottle responsible for this emotional excess. How could anyone *not* love such a man?

"Help me, Brandon," she said recklessly, choking on her tears. "It's all so hopeless. Such a terrible, awful mess. I don't know what I'm going to do."

CHAPTER FIVE

"FIRST YOU NEED to relax." Sitting beside her on the bed, Brandon took her trembling hand in his steady one. Tilting her chin with his other hand, he gave her the same calm look of affectionate reassurance she had so often seen him turn on Ginny. As she stared at him, his warmth wrapped around her like a blanket, and miraculously her tears slowed in their tracks.

"That's right," he said, his voice gentling her. Still clasping her hand, he put his other arm across her shoulders and pulled her up against his chest. "That's the way, now, sweetheart. Take it easy. Everything is going to be all right."

Incredible how different one word could sound. When Douglas had called her "sweetheart," it had been a degradation. Yet the word fell from Brandon's lips like a balm.

Obediently, she shut her eyes and took a shuddering breath. She must have had more to drink than she realized, because as soon as her eyes closed she felt a curious floating sensation, as if she were there but not there, rocking in a dark half-world created by alcohol and exhaustion. But she did feel better. There was a magic in this man, she thought as she let herself float freely, feeling his hand stroking her arm. He had merely to promise that everything would be all right, and believing him, she felt every tense muscle in her body relax. Even the storm outside seemed pacified. The thunder subsided to a muted rumble; the wind dropped to a lull.

"Now tell me about it," he whispered. "Tell me why you want to leave."

"I don't want to. I *have* to," she said, but it ended with something like a whimper, and she pressed her cheek against his collar. She didn't want to think about Douglas, or her father, or anything. She wanted to hide here in Brandon's arms, her eyes shut and reality a million miles away.

As if sensing that her fear was escalating, he held her more tightly, bringing her close enough to feel the steady thumping of his heart against her breast.

"It's okay, Kelsey. Whatever it is, we can work it out. Just tell me. Tell me why you think you have to leave."

"It's Douglas," she said finally, though as she had feared, the name sent an ominous ripple through the fragile peace she'd found. Brandon's hand stilled on her arm and his heartbeat stopped briefly. When it resumed, the beat had changed, losing the perfect constancy that had been so reassuring.

"Douglas?" Brandon didn't take his arm away, but she sensed that he wanted to. Her hand crept blindly to his chest. "I thought he was in San Francisco."

"He is. But I just called him." Her voice was low. "He's coming home. He should be here in two hours. He's coming because...because I told him...I told him I won't marry him."

Brandon pulled away from her fractionally, and she clutched at his shirt with a blind panic. "Don't be angry," she begged. "I can't. I can't marry him."

"Oh, my God." Slowly, using the heels of his hands, Brandon held her at arm's length. "Look at me," he said, and reluctantly she lifted her tear-filled eyes to his. It was full night now, and the only light in the room was a faint silver glow from the landscaping globes three stories below them.

"Brandon, please . . ."

Now that they were no longer clasped heart to heart, their magic circle of safety was broken, and the storm seemed to know it. A whip-crack of thunder and lightning split the room, illuminating Brandon's ashen face, and the wind howled through the window.

Brandon didn't seem to feel the cold. Perhaps his shirt offered more protection than her scrap of flimsy silk. Her own back tingled, and shivers ran up and down her spine.

Still he searched her face, though she wondered what he could hope to see in this bleak, gray darkness.

"Brandon, what's wrong?" Her voice shook. "Are you angry?"

"Why did you do it?" To her relief, he didn't sound angry. He sounded . . . what? Without any facial expression to guide her, she could hardly decide what to name the emotion that thickened his voice. "Why can't you marry him?"

"I don't love him," she said, amazed to find how simple it turned out to be. "I can't marry a man I don't love. It's just as you said, Brandon. It's all wrong."

His hands tightened painfully on her shoulders. "Is that why?" He sucked in a sharp breath. "What happened today—between us . . . Is that why you decided not to marry Douglas?"

She shook her head, aware that her answer was very important. This was her decision. He shouldn't have to carry any of the blame. "No," she said. "No, that's not why."

But he didn't seem convinced. His grip didn't relax, and her shoulders began to ache under his punishing fingers.

"Because that should never have happened," he went on, as if she hadn't answered him. A series of lightning flashes, quick and erratic, illuminated the room in disjointed bursts, and in that strange light she finally saw how tense he was, how sad his eyes, how grim his mouth.

"I was coming in here to tell you that," he continued when darkness returned. "To say I was sorry." He opened and closed his fingers convulsively, squeezing her shoulders. "I *am* sorry, Kelsey. It was just... just something I couldn't control."

"I know," she said, staring at her hands in her lap. They looked like a ghost's hands, disembodied, dim and filmy.

A gust of the fitful wind tossed the first pellets of rain against the windowsill. With a muffled groan, he wrenched himself away and stood up.

He moved to the window, staring out into the wild night, and then he shoved the window down, slamming it against the sill. Immediately a barrage of staccato rain set up an angry, thwarted clacking against the glass.

"Kelsey, listen. I promise you it won't ever happen again," Brandon said, still standing at the window, his back to the bed. "You don't need to run away from it—from me. I'll leave. Tomorrow morning. Right away. I swear I never meant to come between you and Douglas—"

"You didn't," she broke in miserably.

"Of course I did. Do you think I haven't seen what was happening between us? It's been driving me crazy. I should have left a long time ago—"

"No," she insisted, unable to bear the note of self-recrimination in his voice. "You don't have to leave. It's not your fault. What happened today didn't make any difference."

"Didn't make any difference?" As if she had slapped him, his words exploded from him with a retaliatory fury. "Didn't make any *difference?*" With three violent paces he crossed the room and knelt on the bed behind her, one strong thigh on either side of her hips. He grabbed her shoulders again and shook her in a rough anger.

"Be honest with yourself, Kelsey," he said into her ear. "We wanted each other. Badly. If we'd been alone, I would have made love to you right there in the dirt. And you would have let me."

She winced, mortified and yet unable to deny it. *"Brandon,"* she pleaded, but he didn't show any mercy. His hands held her prisoner while his words beat at her like a hailstorm.

"And it's not the first time, is it? What about at the picnic? I was so weak from wanting you I thought I'd drown." His fingers tightened. "And every night, every blessed night for weeks I've gone by your door, and each time it's as if something is tearing at my gut, pulling me into this room."

She lowered her face into her hands, unable to bear the raw honesty in his words. It had been bad enough to believe she had been alone in the wanting. Now, to know he felt it, too. . . .

"All that has made a hell of a difference to me," he said bitterly. "It's turned my whole damn world upside down."

She didn't turn around. She didn't want to see the anger on his face, or for him to see the emotions that must have been as blatant as a brand on her own features.

Instead, she tried to think. How could she make him understand things she barely understood herself? It was a subtle distinction, yet such an important one. She couldn't marry Douglas because she didn't love him. The fact that she *did* love Brandon had everything and nothing to do with it.

But she couldn't say that. It sounded illogical, twisted. Words were such slippery, disappointing things. They could never capture the shape and texture of passion, never map the intricate boundaries of love.

She shook her head in exhausted confusion.

"I'm sorry," she said numbly. "Maybe it will be all right when I'm gone. Maybe your world will straighten out again."

He laughed, but the laughter was black, and the grip of his hands on her shoulders tightened. She would have bruises the next day.

"Is that what you really believe?" He made a wordless noise that was as full of angry pain as the growl of a trapped animal. "Well, let me tell you what *I* think. I think..."

For a minute she thought he was going to lose control, but then, with a groan, the anger seemed to drain out of him. He dropped his head onto her shoulder, burying his face in her hair.

"I think..." His breath came hard and fast, and it sent shivering waves rippling down her back. "God help me, Kelsey, I think my world will *end* if you go."

His words were shockingly open and vulnerable, filled with a ravaged passion. Stunned, she tried to stand, though she knew her legs would never hold her. "No." His hands held her down, and his knees tightened, locking her between his legs in a dizzying embrace. She could feel the rigid thrust of his body against her back. "Don't leave me, sweetheart. Please don't leave me."

His voice was anguished, and in it she heard the same engulfing need that racked her own body. Still, she writhed impotently, unable to free herself even so much as an inch. She *had* to go. Now—before it was too late.

But it was already too late. Her frantic wriggling had loosened her robe until it opened and slid down her arms. Suddenly his lips were burning a hot path over her bare skin.

She was lost. A turbulent churning roiled deep inside her, racing through her, then doubling back on itself and intensifying, like a tidal wave caught in a bottle. Brandon's lips continued to advance, crossing her shoulder blades with their icy fire, urging the robe out of the way, inching the fabric down across her breasts until only her nipples were covered.

But the cloth would only go so far. The knot in her sash held tightly, and the robe became a silken bond, pinioning her elbows to her sides. With a low sound of frustration, his lips rose along her spine, between her shoulder blades, up her neck—dragging a scalding geyser of sensation up from her molten core.

"Turn around," he whispered, but she just shook her head. She wasn't ready to face him yet, to admit, gaze to gaze, how much she wanted this.

He seemed to understand and didn't insist. His mouth found her ear, nipping and tasting and whispering, each hot breath shooting like a fiery arrow through her. His hands slid over her shoulders and then slipped down over her bare skin, toward the rounded swell of her breasts. With one decisive wrench he pulled apart the sides of her robe, from neck to knee, opening her to him completely.

Her body gleamed in the dim light, and his low moan shook with an unsteady mixture of need and awed reverence.

"You'll never know how often I've dreamed of this," he said, tracing his fingers over the soft flesh, brushing his thumbs across the hard nipples. Her head fell back, and a whimper floated out from her lips. Oh, yes, she was lost. They were both lost now.

"Kelsey," he whispered, his breath rough and shallow against her ear. His touch was growing firmer, more insistent. "I don't know what's right and what's wrong anymore." He held her nipples lightly between thumb and forefinger, tantalizing with the promise of an exquisite pain.

"I only know I can't settle for the dream. I have to have you now."

She didn't answer. She couldn't. But she didn't stop him, either, and that was its own answer.

His fingers closed over the aching peaks, until daggers of light seemed to drive through her from breast to hip. Just when she thought she could stand no more, the touch turned into a kneading, and she arched against him, unable to bear the delicious misery without moving, yet unable to ask him to stop.

But when, after a minute, his hands left her breasts, drifting down her rib cage toward her stomach, she murmured a frantic protest. She wasn't ready. The touch he wanted seemed suddenly too intimate, too dangerous. She tried to gather her robe together in fists that were trembling. "Brandon—"

"It's all right, my love," he whispered into her neck as his fingers continued their inexorable slide. For just a second, her heart stopped. *My love.* Uttered in his hypnotic voice, the word was like a comet trailing a starry path across the sky. *My love.*

"It's all right," he repeated softly. Deftly unknotting the sash that still circled her waist, he found the flat, quivering planes of her stomach and drew fiery circles with his fingertips.

"Is it?" she asked tremulously, gasping as his hands spun lower still, spiraling along her inner thighs. "Is it really?"

"It has to be," he said thickly, and she heard the catch in his voice. With just two feather-light fingers he nudged her legs apart, as if she were a puzzle whose secret he knew by heart. "Nothing that feels this good could possibly be wrong."

And he was right. She knew it the instant his fingers found her. So achingly, blindingly right. She moaned and shifted slightly. His fingers belonged on her. In her. She moaned again and shut her eyes.

Without thinking she opened farther, leaning back, locking her arms around his neck as he worked his magic. How strange that she had been afraid! She had nothing to hide from him. He already knew her secrets, knew all the hidden places where her dreams lay, waiting to be set free. He knew all her tiny fears and the murmuring syllables that would make them disappear. He knew, too, the mysterious rhythms and the delicate pressures that would propel her to the edge of sanity, and how to bring her back before she fell, only to push her there again....

Soon there would be no turning back, and she began to long for that final fall. Instead of passively accepting whatever pleasures his fingers offered her, she began to beg, with small noises, for more.

"Wait," he said suddenly, and she realized that his fingers had stopped. She rocked slightly against them, caught in the yearning, needing the release they had promised her.

"Not yet," he said, somehow denying her without removing his hands. "I want to see you."

She made a small cry of frustration, but by keeping his hands absolutely still, he managed to quiet the violent throbbing that had been building inside her. She felt the demanding need back off a pace and drew a shaky breath.

He removed his hands slowly, careful not to jar the precarious balance. "Lie down," he said, backing away from her, still on his knees. "Let me look at you."

With slow hands he eased her down onto the bed, positioning one leg on either side of him so that he knelt before her. "Now," he said, his voice full of promise as his hands stroked up her legs. "I can see how beautiful you are."

His eyes glittered in the silver light, and he slid off the bed slowly. Standing just inches from her, he began to undress.

One button at a time, he opened his shirt—and, oh, there were so many buttons! It was as if he could stretch time, making the simple act of undressing an act of torture. But finally the shirt was discarded. And the sight of his torso, so broad and clean and strong, was almost more than she could bear.

"Hurry," she breathed, trying to slow the heavy thudding of her heart, the tight coiling of her muscles.

When he stood naked before her, she couldn't speak at all. In spite of everything that had happened between them, in spite of every vivid dream, she was unprepared for the reality of him—the overpowering masculinity, the raw sexuality, the sheer heartbreaking beauty.

As he knelt over her once again, positioning all that glorious strength between her legs, tears filled her eyes and fell into her hair. She had never dared to dream that he would come to her like this.

Somehow he misinterpreted both the silence and the tears. Holding himself back with visible effort, he took her hand and held it to his chest.

"Is this what you want, Kelsey?" he asked, and she could tell by the tripping of his heart how much courage it took him to ask. She could feel the hardness of him pressing against her, seeking the place where, of all places, it belonged. One shift of her body, one slight lift, and all the waiting would be over.

When she didn't answer right away, his heart stumbled beneath her hand. "Kelsey?" he said again, his forehead glistening with perspiration and his desperation palpable in his voice. "Do you want this?"

What should she say? Was he, at this eleventh stroke of midnight, passing the decision—and the responsibility—to her? Was he offering her one last chance to save them both from something he knew could ultimately bring nothing but pain? He was passion's prisoner right now, but what about later? Later, when the guilt set in, or the shame. Later, when he realized he had made love to the woman his brother planned to marry. Later, when he might find it more convenient to blame her than to blame himself. Later, when his disgust might well break her heart.

But she let the chance drift by untaken. Maybe it was the wine, or maybe it was the desire that had accumulated unacknowledged in her over these past weeks like a fire that raged unseen behind a closed door, growing more awesome and uncontrollable with every passing minute.

Or maybe it was magic. The simple, wonderful magic that was Brandon had taken her past caution, beyond fear. She was in love, and there was nothing she wouldn't give to this man.

Being in his arms was her dream, too, and just for tonight, the dream was the only thing that mattered. Maybe, just maybe, it would be so wonderful he would never regret it.

For an answer she repeated his words. "Nothing that feels this good could possibly be wrong," she whispered, lifting her hips to him.

And so, with all his magic and all her dreams, he took her. He entered her tenderly, but tenderness was too fragile a bloom to exist in the wild climate of their desire. With a low cry, she locked her legs around his back, pressing him into her as far as she could. He groaned with relief, finally understanding that she didn't need, didn't want, heroic restraint.

He offered her his passion, instead, driving into her with a force that shook her soul. She held him tightly, her fingers digging into his sweat-slicked back as he pounded into her, over and over, calling her name in an agony of possession.

Outside, the thunder that had been silent for so long returned with a vengeance. It roared through the room, masking their moans as they forced each other to more intense sensations, to greater heights and ever more dangerous pinnacles.

And then, as they reached the limits of pleasure and pain together, the thunder smothered their shuddering cries of surrender. Unable to stop themselves, they spiraled off the earth in a thrilling plunge that seemed to last forever.

But afterward, as she lay in his arms, trying to put together the pieces of her shattered soul, the thunder wasn't quite loud enough to hide his words from her—or to soften the guilty misery with which he spoke them.

"Kelsey," he said, as if he was only half-restored and didn't fully know what he was saying. "Oh, Kelsey, Kelsey, what have we done?"

CHAPTER SIX

THEY LAY TOGETHER, not yet ready to let go, allowing their bodies to say a hundred tender things that their voices didn't have the words for. He traced the curve of her hip; she followed the muscled hollow between his ribs. He touched a softening nipple with his palm; she brushed her lips against his navel. He breathed deeply, his face buried in her hair; she sighed into his ear.

But soon, too soon, she felt reality slither back into the room. It came silently, but its presence altered everything. Gradually Brandon's legs unwound themselves from hers, his cocooning arms fell back against the sheets, his nuzzling head dropped against the pillow. They were, once again, two people.

"We'd better get dressed," he said, and she clung to the misty reluctance she heard in his thickened voice. He didn't want to go—she could hear that.

She didn't answer, and for a long minute he lay with his eyes shut, not moving or speaking. But then, with an effort she could almost feel, he sat up and swung his feet over the edge of the bed, turning his back to her. Clearing his throat, he ran his hands through his hair. "We'd better hurry," he said over his shoulder.

That sounded much firmer, and she was amazed at how quickly he seemed able to reclaim himself. She still felt as if she were made of clouds, unformed, unearthly, incapable of any motion except weightless floating.

"Come back," she whispered. She needed his breath against her, the silent urgings of his hands. She was the cloud, she thought dreamily, and he was her wind.

But instead, a soft creaking told her he was rising. She lay there helplessly and watched as he began to put on his clothes. He didn't speak, didn't look at her, until, apparently sensing her unnatural immobility, he said in a hoarse voice, "I can't. We have to hurry, sweetheart."

The endearment lacked the buoyant magic he had given it earlier, more perfunctory than passionate. The cloud of her spirits gathered a heavy weight and began to sink. Pulling the sheets up to her chin, she curled into a ball. "Why?"

He had already slipped into his jeans, and now he was shrugging his arms into his shirt. The long row of buttons, which had taken so achingly long to release, seemed to close up with ironic speed. The bed jostled as he dropped back onto it and bent over to retrieve his shoes and socks.

"Why?" She stared at the back of the crisp white shirt that seemed so unaffected by what had passed between them.

"We've got to get out of here," he said. His voice was unfamiliar and strained. "I'm taking you home. But hurry, Kelsey. We haven't got much time."

"Time? You mean before Douglas comes back?"

He finally turned to face her, shoving his shirttails into his jeans. "Of course I mean before Douglas comes back. Do you want him to find us like this?" She was grateful for the watery darkness, which masked his expression. "I'll bring the car around. Meet me downstairs in five minutes."

He was almost at the door before she found her voice. "Wait!" He stopped, but his body was tight with tension. "Maybe I shouldn't run away, Brandon," she said hesitantly. She wasn't really sure what he was thinking, nor whether he was angry with her or with himself. "Maybe I should stay and talk to Douglas now."

He turned stiffly. "And tell him what?" His voice was flat, uncompromising.

"Tell him—" she swallowed hard "—just what I've already told him, that I can't marry him. That he can't do anything to change my mind."

"No," he said in that same curious tone. "I don't want you to make any final decisions tonight. Go home and think it over before you say things you'll regret."

"I don't *need* to think it over!" she cried, sitting up, clutching the linens to her breast. Why was he talking like this? Did he really believe she might even now change her mind and marry his brother? "I'll never regret it," she said more quietly, hoping he knew what she meant. She had made two irrevocable decisions tonight, and she wouldn't regret either of them, no matter what happened now. "When you first came in here, I told you I had already made my final decision."

"I know." His voice was still resolute, but somewhere, buried under that unemotional monotone, was a pain so sharp that if exposed might prove lethal. "But I don't think you were in any condition to decide anything. You'd had quite a lot to drink. And after what happened during the football game... Well, it had put a lot of pressure on you, might have...confused you."

"I wasn't confused," she said firmly. "I can't marry Douglas because of how I feel about *him*—not how I feel about *you*. He and I had already talked before you came in here. We had the most horrible fight—"

"That's exactly what I mean," he broke in. "A fight. Every couple fights, but they get over it, make up and go on. I didn't give you time to do that tonight, Kelsey. I didn't give you time to think."

She was beside herself with frustration. Why was he refusing to understand? "I don't *need* to think!"

"But *I* need you to do just that. Can't you see? I don't want to be responsible..." With an impatient sigh he waved away her repeated protest. "I know you say I'm not, but these things—" he gestured toward the bed "—these things have a way of muddying the issues, of making even rational people do irrational things."

"These things?" She was rigid with disbelief. His tone was so impersonal. "Do you mean *sex?* Do you mean that just because we made love I can't think straight?"

"God, Kelsey...I don't know." He ran his hand through his fair hair violently. "Maybe I mean that *I* can't."

Her heart sank. He couldn't have been more explicit. He wasn't really worried about her state of mind. *He* was the one who needed time to think. He wasn't sure what he felt for her—if, indeed, he felt anything—and he didn't want to decide right now. He wanted to clear his conscience, be assured that he hadn't wrecked his brother's relationship.

"Kelsey." Finally a note of warmth crept back into his voice. "This all happened pretty fast for you, sweetheart. I'm trying to do the right thing here, trying to give you time..."

"Yes. Of course," she said quietly. Turning her back to him, she reached for her robe. "I'll be down in five minutes."

She was down in four, small suitcase in hand, and he was already waiting, his silver sports car pulled up in front of the porch, where she could climb in without getting wet.

As soon as she pulled the door shut he gunned the engine, and the car shot out of the driveway. And thus, in mutual guilt and silence, they began their race toward tragedy....

THE MEMORIES WERE STILL strong the next day as Kelsey
stared out the window of Brandon's bedroom. She brushed
the palm of her hand restlessly over the velvety petals of a
chrysanthemum, hardly feeling the soft tickle, barely
smelling the shiver of perfume. Her eyes and her mind were
firmly focused on the view below her.

From the vantage point of this second-story tower window she could follow the drive, which looked like a white
ribbon lain across the green lawn, all the way to the mouth
of Cliff Road.

Where were they? Greg Siddons and Ginny had headed
for the hospital hours ago, the back seat of the car piled high
with pillows until it had reminded Kelsey of a king's litter,
in which Brandon would be carried home in splendid comfort.

"Don't fret, honey. They'll be here soon." Frances spoke
from the doorway, and Kelsey whipped around. She must
have looked strange, because Frances's eyes narrowed, and
crossing the room briskly, she joined Kelsey in the circular
alcove. With a cool hand she patted Kelsey's face.

"Not to worry," Frances said with a firm smile. "You
know hospitals. They're probably not quite through emp-
tying his pockets to pay the bill. They wouldn't want to miss
a single nickel."

With some effort Kelsey returned the smile, rallying to
Frances's bolstering tone. She was going to have to pull
herself together. She couldn't go around with her nerves all
jagged and exposed like this, fearing disaster around every
corner.

"Are they finished in there?" Kelsey inclined her head
toward the adjoining room. Workmen had been laboring
since dawn, transforming it into a mini health spa.

"Yes." Frances sighed. "Finally. But what a to-do! And
why it had to be done this morning I'll never know. You

can't tell me Mr. Brandon is going to come straight home from the hospital and start pounding iron.''

Kelsey smiled again, this time with more genuine amusement. "*Pumping* iron," she corrected mildly. "And I certainly hope not." She remembered how battered Brandon had looked. "I hope Dr. James will make him take it easy."

"Poof!" The sound Frances made dismissed the doctor. "Not likely. Dr. J. hasn't been able to make that boy do *anything* since he was twelve years old. We'll be lucky if he doesn't dash right off to dig up mummies in Bolivia."

"I don't think they have mummies in Bolivia," Kelsey said with a grin, though the crinkles at the edges of Frances's eyes told her the housekeeper knew it perfectly well. "Besides, until those bandages come off his eyes—"

She stopped suddenly and, unable to meet the reflection of her own fear in Frances's expression, dropped her gaze and stepped out of the alcove to take a final look around the bedroom. Bedecked in flowers, freshly dusted and polished, the room smelled and looked wonderful. But Brandon wouldn't be able to see it.

"How about in here?" Frances stalked over to the king-size bed and took an efficient swat at the pillows. "Did you bring everything in?"

Kelsey picked up a stack of Brandon's jeans and slipped them into the bureau drawer reluctantly, smoothing them with a lingering hand. "I think so," she said. "This was the last."

At Brandon's request—sent via Greg Siddons—Kelsey had transferred Brandon's things from the room he had been occupying to this second-floor tower suite. Each floor of the Traherne house had a tower suite: one very large room in the center, with a lovely circular alcove formed by the tower, a luxurious bath, and two smaller rooms that flanked

the main area. Until last week, this one had belonged to
Douglas.

"They're here!"

Coming to with a jolt, Kelsey shoved the drawer shut with
her hip and followed Frances back to the alcove. Sure
enough the rental car was easing to a stop at the front door
below them.

Before the engine was quite silenced, Ginny popped like
an overwound jack-in-the-box from the car. Her happy
voice bubbled up to the open window where Kelsey stood,
suddenly paralyzed, watching as the little girl yanked on the
door to the back seat.

"Come on, come on," Ginny urged, her hands stretched
out as if to drag her brother from the car if necessary.

"Patience, pesky," Brandon's tolerant voice responded
from somewhere in the pillowed depths of the back seat.
"My ribs aren't nearly as excited about this as you are."

But Ginny kept cheerleading, and slowly Brandon
emerged. First just a long leg, then another, then his bandaged hand against the door for balance. And then, finally,
with a strain that whitened his knuckles, he stood up.

Kelsey hadn't realized she was holding her breath until she
heard it come out in a low *whoosh*. Brandon was home.
Somehow she hadn't quite believed it would happen until
this very moment.

And, miraculously, he was as magnificent as ever. A lean
and muscular six-two, he had the golden grace of a man who
worked and played outdoors, pursuing both with an equally
intense satisfaction. A week in the hospital had dimmed but
not destroyed his honey tan, and even the painful caution
with which he stood couldn't make that perfectly propor-
tioned body awkward.

The wind blew his slacks against his legs—oh, he was too
thin, wasn't he?—and lifted fair, wavy hair from his brow,

sadly crisscrossed with half-healed cuts, discolored at the temples with the fading echoes of bruises.

Dr. James had done his job well: there would be very little scarring. But there was something else, some new mark of maturity, which, while no less attractive, was somehow heartrending. The unmistakable brand of suffering. It would be in his eyes, too.

But she couldn't see his eyes. Finally allowing herself to focus on the strip of bandage that circled his head, Kelsey sagged against the window. In the hospital, the blindness had seemed just another medical indignity. Here, in the sunshine, in his own front yard, it was an abomination.

As if he had heard something, Brandon lifted his face blindly toward them. The pain had left its mark on the rest of his face, too. His cheekbones stood out starkly over tight hollows. His lips, which had once curved naturally upward as if perpetually poised to smile, were shockingly flat, disappearing at each end into shadowed lines that hadn't been there before.

"Oh, no," she said. "Oh, Brandon."

"Steady." Frances squeezed Kelsey's elbow, nudging her erect. She spoke quietly, so that her voice wouldn't carry down to the others. "It's steady they're going to need right now."

Kelsey shook her head. Steady? How? She felt like two people—one who wanted to race down the staircase and anoint his wounds with kisses and laughter, and one who wanted only to slump to the floor and weep.

"It'll come," the housekeeper said quietly. "But it's going to take a little time. And a little courage." She took Kelsey's hand. "You can do it. You're not one of those lily-hearted girls who can't say boo to a duck."

"Lily-livered," Kelsey corrected automatically.

"Liver?" Frances grimaced. "Ugh. Still, I'm right. You're a stout-livered young woman, so you hang on and, when the time comes, go take the lion by the horns."

"Stout-*hearted,*" Kelsey began, wondering if she could sort out all the metaphors, but finally she saw the twinkle in Frances's eye. Maybe she *was* overreacting. Maybe all it would take was patience and gumption—and, of course, that amazing horned lion. She smiled, just a little, as the tightness in her chest began to ease.

"Okay, okay," she said. "I'll try."

But just then they heard Brandon's halting footsteps on the stairs and, in spite of Frances's vote of confidence, Kelsey realized she felt rather lily-hearted, after all.

KELSEY WAS IN THE ROOM. He knew it the moment he limped through the door.

Even through the barrage of overripe roses and decaying daisies, he could smell her perfume. What was it about that scent of lilacs that was so arousing? No woman he'd ever known before had worn it.

It shouted her presence as loudly as if he could see her standing there. And it wasn't because his sense of smell was compensating for his lack of vision. He didn't believe in that, and even if such compensation did happen, it wasn't going to happen to him. He wasn't going to be blind long enough to do any compensating. Dr. James was going to take the bandages off in two days, and Brandon absolutely refused to consider the possibility that his eyes would not be healed.

No. This was nothing new. He had often known when Kelsey was nearby. Some atavistic tingling along his spinal cord, some primal awareness that tickled his tailbone, had alerted him. And then the damn perfume had drifted into his brain, making him think of things like…well, just things you didn't think about your brother's fiancée.

For the next few minutes, Ginny dragged him across the room, pointing out every flower as if he hadn't spent the past week smelling the wretched things. As if the smell of flowers hadn't become synonymous with hospitals and rage and pain.

He tried not to disappoint his sister, listening to her rhapsodies with as much enthusiasm as he could muster, but, God, he was getting tired. He wasn't used to the crutch yet, and it was digging mercilessly into his armpit and bruising the heel of his hand. His knee, where the tendons were strained, was aching in big red waves of pain, and he wanted desperately to sit down.

But he hated to frighten Ginny, who seemed so pathetically eager for reassurance. So he kept walking and tried to keep the pain off his face.

"Ginny, honey, I think you should let Brandon sit down now." Kelsey sounded worried, as though she'd seen through his facade of manly stoicism. And suddenly, perversely, he wouldn't have sat down for all the gold in Tut's tomb.

"No," he said flatly. "I'm fine. I'm better standing up."

This was met with skeptical silence all around, but at least Kelsey didn't insist. She didn't say another word, and he could only wonder where she was, how she looked, how she'd arranged her long, thick hair, even what she was wearing.

Maybe one of the tailored skirts she always wore to the office with Douglas? Or was she in her favorite weekend getup, those snug blue jeans and that cotton shirt, the one with a long row of tiny buttons down the front?

Either way, he was almost glad he couldn't see her. She was equally seductive in both.

But what the hell was he thinking about Kelsey's clothes for? If there was anything good to be said for being blind as a bat, it was that he didn't have to struggle to keep his eyes off Kelsey Whittaker's body. Now if someone could just blind him to these mental pictures...

"All right, now, enough about the flowers." Frances's voice broke into his frustrated thoughts, and he welcomed the intrusion. "Come on down to the kitchen and get a glass of apple juice, Ginny, while Brandon rests his leg a little."

He felt Ginny's hand clutch his even more tightly, as if she was afraid to leave him even for a minute in case he went up in a puff of smoke, never to be seen again. Much as Douglas had done. Their parents, too, though Ginny had been too young to remember that. He squeezed back. Poor kid. She had lived through a lot for such a little thing.

But she had to learn to trust again sometime, and since he couldn't drag this miserable leg down the stairs again for love or money or apple juice, now was a good time to start.

"Go ahead, pesky. I'll be here when you get back." He took a hobbling step and gestured with the crutch. "Old Peg Leg Traherne is going to be pretty easy to find for quite a while."

"Good, then." Frances pried Ginny's fingers loose. He heard a jumble of footsteps heading for the door. "You'd better stay here, Kelsey," Frances added firmly.

"Stay? But Brandon needs to rest." Kelsey's voice sounded rushed and high.

"Well, lead him to a chair, then. You two need to talk. You're the only one who knows where you put everything in this room, so you've got to give him the deluxe tour."

The silence that stretched between the two women virtually vibrated, and Brandon wondered what it meant. What looks and gestures were passing between them? What communications were mouthed so that he would not understand? His helplessness infuriated him, and combined with the pain, it was more than he could bear.

"Let's get on with it, then," he said. "Is it asking too much for somebody to tell me where a damn chair is?"

Another shocked silence met his unreasonable command, but this time it was in response to *his* words, and he felt a gratifying sense of control regained.

"Of course not," Kelsey said at last, sounding diffident, and he heard her move across the room. "I'll show you."

He held out his free arm, surprised at himself, stunned at how much anger seemed to be lying just below the surface, shocked at how good it felt to hear that submissive tone in her voice. God, what was happening to him? He hadn't ever been sadistic before, had he? What had Kelsey done to make him feel so...so savage whenever she was around?

And why, when she placed her soft fingers on his arm to guide him toward the chair, was her touch like fire? Why did he want to whip around and shake her until she screamed, and at the same time want with a raw, animal need to throw her onto the bed—wherever that was—and make love to her until she cried?

Bullets of sweat stood out on his forehead as he sank onto the chair.

What the hell had happened that night?

CHAPTER SEVEN

"I PUT ALL THE SWEATERS in the left-hand tier of closet drawers," Kelsey wound up ten minutes later, trying not to sound as relieved as she felt. It had been a long ten minutes.

"I tried to stick as much as possible to the system you were using, but this room is much bigger—I hope it's not confusing."

He didn't even turn his head. "I'm sure it'll be fine."

That was typical of his responses throughout—more expansive, in fact, than most. Monosyllabic grunts were all he had managed at first, but pain could have accounted for that. He was obviously suffering. His skin glistened with perspiration; his lips were tight lines edged in white.

For Kelsey, standing in impotent misery on the other side of the room, watching was torture. Gripping the rim of the dresser, she had somehow stifled the urge to go to him. His very posture seemed to forbid any such overture.

Gradually the pain seemed to pass, but though his grunts grew into words, his manner never really thawed. He seemed to be enduring her presence the same way he bore his physical discomfort—in grim silence.

Well, she thought with a flicker of the confusing anger that had been lurking at the edge of her consciousness all week, it would be easy enough to fix that. She had at least a dozen other things calling her—including some important real-estate reports she needed to read before Friday's meeting with Mr. Farnham.

"This must have been a lot of work," he said, surprising her with both the length and the courtesy of his sentence. "I didn't mean to trouble you. I thought Frances would do it."

"Oh, it was no trouble at all," she said stiltedly, sounding like something out of an etiquette book. Burden her? Didn't he know? She would do so much more than this for him. She would do *anything*.

Immediately her annoyance was forgotten, replaced by a spark of hope, and she suddenly saw her anger for what it was—a flimsy shield thrown up over raw wanting. And it took so little to breach it—a polite tone, a slight loosening of those tight lips, a tiny movement in her direction, and she was there, rushing to accept whatever crumb fell her way.

Humiliating, really. And yet he didn't sound quite as cold now. Perhaps, even if he couldn't remember details, he remembered something—some echo of a warmth between them, some half-remembered joy in being together.

"Frances was busy with the gym," she went on quickly, reluctant to let a long pause destroy the momentum. "But they finally got everything built. It's like he-man heaven in there, Brandon. You should see it."

"I'd like to," he said dryly, but there was a potent frustration behind the sarcasm, and for just an instant, before he forced it back to his lap, his hand jerked toward his head, as if he might rip away the bandages.

She flushed and bit her lip, wishing the words unspoken. How tactless—and yet the phrase was just one of those things people always said.

"You *will* see it, Brandon," she said fervently. He looked, not pitiful—never that—but tragic, all that golden glory caged, all the force of his incredible personality chained to the chair by just one tiny roll of white gauze bandages.

But not forever. Surely not forever. There was so much power in him. Surely that fierce vitality, that aura of imminent rage, would simply *force* his body to heal.

"You'll see again," she said. "I'm sure of it."

"Are you really?" He tilted his chin, giving his face the same touch of skepticism his voice held. "Impressive. Are you using tarot cards or tea leaves?"

She knew, in some intellectual way, that it wasn't really Brandon talking. It was just the bereavement and the frustration. Still, his sarcasm stung. She flushed again and turned to leave the room.

"I'll go check on Ginny," she said brusquely, annoyed that her voice shook. "I'll make up a list and leave it with Frances, so if there's anything you can't find—"

"Where were we going, Kelsey?"

She halted, her hand on the door, her blood running slow and cold in her veins, like some ice-choked polar stream. Weakly, she stalled, pretending she hadn't heard.

"What?"

"Where were we going?" He sat ramrod straight, his face turned toward her. She had the eerie feeling he could see through the bandages, that he could see to the fear that dragged at her insides, giving her this empty feeling.

This was the moment she had been dreading, the moment she would have to give him some explanation. Over and over during the past week she'd asked herself what she could say, all the while praying that she wouldn't have to tell him, that somehow he would remember on his own.

Now, like a sinkhole opening beneath her feet, the moment had arrived without warning. No time to think of a convincing equivocation. Oh, if only she could speak the truth—ignore Dr. James's orders and pour out her heart, speaking of love and loving, of tears and rain, of commitment and betrayal.

"Don't you remember any part of it, Brandon?"

"No," he said flatly. "I remember playing football with Ginny here at the house just before it got dark. And then I was waking up in the hospital, and it was two days later." He rubbed his hand across his jaw. "It's as if all that time got sucked into a black hole somewhere."

"Yes," she said slowly, stalling while she tried to put the right words together. "Yes, I can see how you must feel."

Standing up, he limped toward the window and propped himself against the sill. With the afternoon sun behind him, his face was cast in shadow. "Well?"

"Well..." she began, dragging the word. "I...well, we—"

"Damn it, Kelsey." He interrupted her halting stammer, his voice as rough as bark. "If you're telling the truth, why the hell are you stalling? And don't bother with anything but the truth." Something dark in his tone made the words sound like a threat. "Just because I can't remember today doesn't mean I won't remember tomorrow."

It was strange, she thought numbly. Looking at him now, silhouetted against the sun, she could almost have mistaken him for the old Brandon. But his words and his tone could never have come from *her* Brandon, the Brandon who had found her here that night, who had kissed away her tears....

What could she say? Obviously he didn't trust her. He'd already decided that her reluctance to talk meant she was concocting a lie. So even if she told him the truth, this disturbing truth that his subconscious mind had rejected and buried, would he believe her?

She tried to imagine it. *I made love to you,* she could say, *but I'd already broken my engagement to Douglas, really I had, so it was not technically a betrayal. And I was prepared to stay here and face Douglas, as angry as I knew he was. You, Brandon, were the one who insisted on driving away in the rain.*

How self-serving it sounded, how convenient! All the suspicion and bitterness in his heart would say she lied.

"You were giving me a ride back to my father's house in San Francisco," she said, deciding with desperate haste that he was right. Only the truth would do—though not necessarily the *whole* truth. "I didn't have a car here."

This was the same thing she'd told the police in the hospital. But the policemen, both young and clearly moved by her appearance of wounded fragility—or perhaps loathe to annoy the respectable, high-tax-bracket families of their elite little town—had accepted the skeletal story. They had tipped their hats and apologized, and urged her to get some rest.

Brandon seemed to have no such chivalrous instincts.

"Home? To San Francisco? Why?" The words were jabs, like a fighter wearing down his opponent with quick thrusts.

"I wanted to see my father," she said.

"Why? It was late. They tell me it was storming."

"I was worried about him," she said, picking through the truth for the safe spots. Don't step there. Or there. But here—maybe it's safe over here. "He...he has problems, you know. He drinks, and sometimes he gambles too much at the track. I'd tried to call him, but he wasn't home. I was worried."

That at least should have a ring of truth. She could hear the trembling in her voice even as she recounted it. Breaking the engagement to Douglas had meant she was abandoning her father. Only that slippery cliff had saved her father, but what a price to pay for salvation!

"Did Douglas know where we were going? Did he know why?"

"No," she said, still sticking to the truth, though her palms had begun to grow moist and her heart had stepped up its pace. "No, I hadn't mentioned I was leaving."

"So what did he think when he saw us driving off together, Kelsey?" Brandon's voice was brutal.

"I don't know," she said weakly, hearing the lie herself, as she was sure he must. But it wasn't really a lie. She *didn't* know.

"Well, what do you *think* was going through his mind?"

When she didn't answer, he cursed and took two abrupt steps toward her before he remembered how handicapped he was. The awareness seemed to enrage him, and though he backed up against the sill again, his voice was tighter than ever. "What the hell *could* he have thought? He thought that you and I—" He broke off, as if he couldn't stand to finish. "And then he died. Damn it, my brother died thinking that I—that you and I..."

His voice trailed off with a strangled sound. Kelsey stared at him, her heart dead in her breast. What could she say? Every word was true, but Dr. James was right—Brandon couldn't face the truth. If she told him now how far their betrayal had really gone, well, he wouldn't believe her. But even if he did it would only make his guilt unendurable.

Perhaps, though, if she told him the truth about her engagement, about Douglas himself.... Clutching at the slim hope, she spoke without thinking.

"Brandon, my relationship with Douglas wasn't..." How could she put this? "It wasn't like a normal engagement. He knew I didn't love him."

"*Everyone* knew you didn't love him," he shot back. "You're a lousy actress. Poor devil. He must have been sick with loving you to take you at that price."

He sounded so bitter that Kelsey's knees threatened to give out from under her. She held on to the dresser with a white-knuckled grip.

"He didn't love me, either, Brandon, not really."

"Didn't love you?" Brandon laughed, a scornful sound that held no mirth at all. "Do you think I never heard him begging at your door? My God, it was enough to melt stone."

She tried to swallow, but her throat felt like sandpaper. She was almost out of courage. The whip of his words had bled her dry, but she had to try one last time.

"That wasn't love. Maybe it was lust. But I think, in some twisted way, it had more to do with power. He wasn't normal—"

"Shut up!" This time he didn't let his blindness stop him. He came barreling out of the alcove, heading straight for her, as if his anger could guide him like a missile to the spot where the enemy stood. "Douglas is dead, and now you think you can come in here with your lies and your excuses? Well, I know my brother, and I know what I heard. If he wasn't 'normal,' it was no wonder. Who would be? You were grinding his heart to bits."

He had, miraculously, found her, and he grabbed her upper arms with fingers of steel. "Don't ever talk to me about Douglas again, Kelsey. Not ever, do you understand?"

She didn't know how she managed to speak, but somehow she did. She heard her voice, mechanical and flat. "Do you want me to move out?"

He wanted to say yes—she could read it in the hard set of his lips, the angry pulse that beat just below his jawline. She could feel it in his fingers as they dug into her soft flesh.

But he didn't let himself say it. "No," he said finally, and there was a world of grudging in the syllable. "There are too many loose ends to tie up and, damn it, I'm in no condition to handle anything yet. You need to close the Farnham deal."

"Someone else can do that," she said stiffly. "Someone else from the office can take over."

"No," he said again, though it was clear he hated to admit that he needed her in any way. "Farnham is crazy about you. Douglas told me how well you manage him, how the old man eats out of your hand." His mouth twisted, as if the idea disgusted him. "And who knows? Given a few more hand-feedings, you might even be able to land yourself a new rich fiancé."

She wrenched her shoulders, trying to pull out of his punishing grasp. How dare he talk to her this way? The Brandon of her dreams was gone indeed, as dead as if he, not his brother, had driven off that cliff.

She spoke with icy pride. "Suppose I don't want to stay?"

"You'll stay, anyway, at least until the deal is signed with Farnham. You owe us that much. You particularly owe it to Ginny. She loves you, and you've got to help her get used to the idea of your leaving. I won't have her hurt again."

She had no answer for that. He was right. Ginny had faced enough loss already. And besides, she didn't want to leave. Not as long as there was hope that Brandon would regain his memory.

But just until the deal was signed with Farnham? If all went well at their next meeting, negotiations wouldn't take more than a few days—a week at the most. Dr. James had warned that it sometimes took months for amnesiacs to recover. If they ever did.

"You'll stay, then," he said. He finally let go of her shoulders, shoving her ever so slightly toward the door.

"But don't ever," he added, his voice regaining some measure of grim control, "mention Douglas's name to me again."

IRONICALLY, THE NEXT person who mentioned Douglas to him was a total stranger.

It was about ten the following morning, and Brandon was sitting in Douglas's office wondering how in hell he was supposed to learn anything about the business when he couldn't read a ledger, couldn't study a blueprint. With his eyes taped shut, he was so helpless he couldn't find the pencils with both hands.

But he had to do *something*. He'd been working out in the gym since dawn. Dr. James had been brutally graphic in his description of what would happen to Brandon's leg if he overdid the exercises, so although Brandon had doubled—okay, tripled—the reps, he realized he couldn't keep it up all day.

So here he was, stuck behind this ridiculous desk, wondering where the pencils were, wondering what he'd do with a pencil if he could find one. He couldn't even doodle, for God's sake.

Kelsey had phoned on the office line early this morning—probably from her bedroom—offering to come in and prep him on the Farnham negotiations, but she sounded as excited about the prospect as a virgin offering to climb on the sacrificial slab. When he'd turned her down, her relief had virtually hummed through the phone lines.

She'd vigorously avoided him since their argument yesterday—once or twice he'd thought he smelled her perfume nearby, but the scent had quickly faded. He could imagine her flitting away, like Beauty fleeing from the Beast, and the image embarrassed him in some obscure way.

He *had* been rather beastly. But hearing her maligning Douglas had provoked him beyond endurance. Douglas, admittedly, had never been the most genial guy in the world—frankly, Brandon had found his personality changed for the worse on this trip home—but if Kelsey disliked him so damn much, she shouldn't have agreed to marry him.

Besides, she was lying. He could hear it in her voice, in the subtle burr that crept into her otherwise pure tones when she was under stress. And he could smell her confusion just as clearly as he could smell her perfume. He could imagine the flush on her cheeks, the tiny frown between her eyebrows, as she searched for a good lie. Ridiculous how he remembered all these details, but not why she'd been in his car that night.

He felt the now-familiar clench of frustration as he made another futile grab for the recollection and came up empty. Breathing deeply, he drummed his fingers on the desktop. Clearly he'd never get the truth from *her*. But she'd better be very careful with those little lies and half-truths. He intended to unearth all those hours from his subconscious, much the way he might once have painstakingly unearthed a valuable piece of Mayan pottery on a dig. And when he did—

Before he could complete his mental threat, the phone rang.

A man's voice asked for Brandon Traherne.

"This is he," Brandon said, his instincts prickling. He had never heard the voice before, but he disliked it immediately.

"Mr. Traherne, this is Al Fuller." The man sounded like a funeral director, Brandon thought, all oily concern and deferential hypocrisy. "I did a great deal of work for your brother. He was one of my best clients and a great man. May I offer my condolences at your loss?"

No, you obsequious bastard, Brandon felt like saying, *you may not.* But that was just the beast in him coming out again, and whoever he was, this Al Fuller didn't deserve to be roared at. Somehow Brandon controlled himself and managed a polite thank-you.

"Yes, well, I'm a private investigator, Mr. Traherne. My firm has worked for your brother for several years."

Brandon was surprised. "A private investigator?" It made no sense. Granted, he had never spent much time learning about ODC over the years—the company was Douglas's baby, and Douglas had made it clear he didn't need and wouldn't welcome Brandon's interference. But still, what use could an office-design company possibly have for a private investigator?

Unless it was personal.

"I'm not surprised you haven't heard of me, Mr. Traherne." Fuller's voice was now amused, and the sound wasn't pleasant. "You wouldn't be hearing from me now if your brother hadn't died. It's a bit awkward, really." But his voice was growing quite jaunty, as if the delicacy of it tickled his funny bone. "After all, you were one of my assignments not long ago."

"Assignments?" Brandon felt a disagreeable crawling sensation across his back. "What does that mean?"

"Oh, just a little job. We had to watch you at the company picnic." He chuckled in a malicious enjoyment of the irony. "I'm still not quite sure what your brother was looking for there. We wrote up the whole day in one paragraph. Boringly wholesome."

Brandon wasn't just surprised anymore. He was stunned. "My brother paid you to follow *me?*"

"Right."

"For God's sake, why?"

"Well, now," Fuller said thoughtfully, "it was kind of a two-for-one, you see. You were with Miss Whittaker, as I recall, and we'd been keeping a bit of an eye on her, too, off and on."

Brandon's first instinct was pure revulsion, and he had to squelch a rather offensive expletive that would have left Mr.

Fuller in no doubt about how the younger Traherne viewed the snooping business. Douglas had been having Kelsey tailed? Somehow that was even more distasteful than the knowledge that Douglas had included Brandon himself in the deal.

How could he? What disloyalties had Douglas suspected her of? Was it business—some kind of corporate hanky-panky? But that was nonsense. Even Douglas at his most paranoid couldn't have believed Kelsey was smuggling lay-out plans for workstations or selling the secret formula for calculating floor loads.

No, Douglas's fears must have been more personal. Brandon's disgust softened into a sort of horrified pity. Of course. Poor Douglas. Because his fiancée turned him away every night with relentless frigidity, he'd begun to fear she was offering her warmth elsewhere.

But the picnic.... Did that mean Douglas suspected Brandon was the one basking in Kelsey's warmth? A wriggling guilt snaked through him as he remembered how much he had enjoyed that day, how intensely he had longed to kiss Kelsey. To be honest, it wasn't any abundance of virtue on his part that had saved them. He'd been burning up with wanting. If Kelsey hadn't pulled away when she had, God only knows what might have happened.

Douglas must not have trusted any man with Kelsey, not even his brother. But then, Douglas knew better than any-one that, though she had a sweet innocence in those wide eyes, Kelsey Whittaker had heartbreaker written all over that luscious body.

And yet, whatever the provocation, Brandon still found it objectionable that Douglas had had her followed. If Douglas couldn't trust her, why would he even *want* to marry her?

He realized belatedly that Fuller was talking.

"I heard your accident has left you in a difficult position," Fuller was saying, "but is there any way you could manage to come to my office today? Mr. Traherne felt it was urgent to get this particular report before tomorrow."

"What?" Having missed the entire first part of Fuller's comment, Brandon was lost. "I'm sorry. What report?"

"I'd rather not discuss it on the telephone," the other man said with slow, unmistakable emphasis. "But I believe you'll find it of crucial value. Isn't there someone who could drive you to my office so that we can talk face-to-face?"

Brandon was suddenly irritated by the exaggerated cloak-and-dagger routine. "Can't you just send me the report by courier?"

"Well," Fuller said, "I thought perhaps, in your condition, you might have a little trouble deciphering it."

A swift anger choked Brandon, as if Fuller had insulted him. Then he forced himself to admit that the man only spoke the truth, unpalatable though it was.

"Well, next week then," he said brusquely. "The doctor's taking the bandages off my eyes tomorrow. I'll read it then."

"Really?" The private detective's tone managed to imply that he thought Brandon might be somewhat overconfident. "Well, perhaps, but this report ought to be seen right away. I can't say any more than that on the telephone. If you'll come to my office—maybe about five o'clock?—I'll be happy to read it to you. I promise you, you'll be very glad you didn't wait."

In spite of himself, Brandon felt the stirrings of curiosity. What could be so important? Tomorrow was Friday. What was happening tomorrow? There was the meeting with Farnham, but surely that wasn't sensitive enough.

A prickling of uneasiness made him sit forward in the chair. Maybe the *next* day, Saturday, was the critical day.

Saturday was to have been Douglas's wedding day. Perhaps this was the final report on Kelsey Whittaker.

"I'll be there," he said, though the words felt strange in his mouth. Did he really want to listen to the furtively gathered details of someone else's life? Of Kelsey's life?

No. If it turned out to be Kelsey, he would simply tell Fuller to throw away the files. Douglas was dead, and the wedding would never take place. Kelsey's rating on the fidelity index was no longer of any interest to anyone.

Unless ... Could the report help him to understand what had happened the night of the accident? Could he resist even the most remote chance to locate another piece of this perplexing puzzle? His mind raced through the possibilities. Had Kelsey known she was being followed? Realizing that some transgression had been exposed, had she decided to scurry away?

He memorized Fuller's address. Surprisingly, it was located on an expensive corner of downtown San Francisco. Obviously Douglas hadn't been Fuller's only client.

Anyway, Greg could drive him. Saying a curt goodbye to Fuller, Brandon called ODC's local branch office and left a message for Greg to pick him up at one. They would get a late lunch in the city. Maybe at his favorite little Chinese place. Surely he could manage an egg roll by himself.

He smiled. The idea of action filled him with the first pleasure he'd felt in a long time. It would do him good to get out of this dismal house, where everyone whispered and hovered and there was nothing to do.

But listening to a report from the oily Mr. Fuller, his conscience nagged, a report gathered by men hiding in bushes...

He cursed aloud, slapping the desk with the palm of his hand. His conscience could just shut up for now. He wasn't going to invade anybody's privacy. Even Kelsey's. He merely needed to get out of the house. Maybe he wouldn't even listen to the blasted report when he got there.

Maybe.

KELSEY GOT THE CALL from ODC's branch office at eleven-thirty. It woke her from a restless catnap she'd been taking, thanks to a miserable sleepless night, and she had to focus hard to understand what the agitated secretary was saying.

Greg Siddons had gone home with stomach flu, which left the office unable to fill Mr. Traherne's request for a driver. Mr. Traherne had said it was important; he needed to go to San Francisco right away. What should they do?

Good question. Looking in her bedroom mirror, Kelsey ran a hand through her tousled hair and tried to think. The branch was too tiny to have any alternatives, and the large main office was in San Francisco, two hours away.

So what should she do? It was a mocking echo of the question that had plagued her all night. In the mirror, Kelsey could see the reflection of her open suitcase. It was empty—she hadn't packed a single dress. Instead, she'd sat awake, thinking and thinking, and thinking some more.

But all the thinking hadn't solidified into anything resembling a decision until right now. Now, with a supernormal clarity, she saw that she was tired of running. Tired of hiding.

Running never solved anything. She, of all people, should know that. She'd spent years helping her father run from his problems and had watched his drinking and gambling grow worse until he was only a shadow of his former self. He'd gone from being merely foolish to being a thief. From a wastrel to a criminal.

Even that hadn't taught her how hopeless denial really was. Rather than make her father face the consequences of his crime, she'd agreed to be a bride of blackmail. And the disaster that had come of it was more horrible than her worst nightmare.

And now here she was, getting ready to run away again. Hadn't she learned anything? Was she really going to follow in her father's footsteps, always afraid to face the pain of reality, pretending everything would be all right tomorrow?

No! The word echoed in her head until it rang.

She loved Brandon Traherne. Whether he was crippled or well, sunny or surly, she loved him. Was she really so spineless that she was going to give up on love so easily? No!

For the first time, she allowed herself to face down the real monster—the worst possible outcome. Maybe the amnesia would be permanent. Maybe Brandon would never remember what had happened that night. What then? Would she give up?

No! He'd learned to care about her once. He'd wanted her once, and perhaps, somehow, he could come to want her again.

But not if she spent the few days she had left huddled in a cowardly heap on this rumpled bed. She stood up straight. The woman in the mirror looked infused with a new and fierce determination.

"I can do it," she said to the secretary, though her voice sounded like a stranger's, and when she met her eyes in the mirror they looked terrified. Somehow make him fall in love with her, as she had fallen in love with him? Was she crazy?

She stared back defiantly. Enough of this cowering fear.

"Don't worry about a thing," she said. "I can handle Brandon."

CHAPTER EIGHT

AS THEY LEFT THE HOUSE, Kelsey maneuvered the hills slowly, always conscious of her silent passenger, careful not to take any sharp turns that might make him nervous. This was, after all, the same road—

"I'm not made of glass, you know," Brandon said suddenly. "You could probably go a little more than five miles an hour without breaking anything."

She glanced over at him, surprised by the ironic smile that played like a shadow at his lips. It was the first time he'd spoken, the first time he'd smiled since—

"Sorry," she said, pressing the accelerator obediently, eager to do whatever made him happy.

Initially she'd feared he would refuse to come at all. When he'd heard that Greg wasn't available, he'd seemed unreasonably frustrated, announcing he would just cancel his appointment. It had taken all her newfound determination, but Kelsey had insisted, logically and calmly, that she was on the payroll and might as well earn her keep. Her work on Mr. Farnham's deal was almost done, ready for the meeting with him tomorrow.

Finally he'd capitulated. "I'm going to see a Mr. Fuller," he said, and his tone had an inexplicable baiting quality, though the name meant nothing to her. "I don't know how long the meeting will take. He has an urgent report for me."

"Well, I'll bring Mr. Farnham's estimates to work on while I wait," she had said mildly, wondering why he sounded combative. "I'll be fine."

"Will you?"

"Of course," she said, confused by his taunting manner. Was he implying that she would resent waiting? But he should know better. He knew she was accustomed to working hard—he had commented more than once on how demanding Douglas seemed to be. Or maybe she was being paranoid again. She wished she could see his eyes. It was maddeningly difficult to try to figure out what he was thinking from just his tone and the set of his mouth.

And until now he had been totally silent—not surly, but locked in private concentration. In the face of such profound distance, her plan to use the afternoon to begin building a new relationship seemed childishly simplistic.

Now, reassured by the lingering half smile, she decided to risk conversation. But what about? What subject was safe? What could she say that wouldn't wipe that long-awaited smile from his lips? She searched her mind as the car descended, sweeping past the crowded, cantilevered houses that clung to the rocky face of the hill, appearing to defy the laws of nature.

Her own position seemed equally precarious; she was clinging to a glimmer of hope, defying the odds, trying to carve her place in an unwelcoming environment.

At least she had the tiny toehold his smile seemed to offer. That was more than she would have dared to hope for yesterday.

"How's it going in the gym?" she asked. Frances had reported with predictable disapproval on Brandon's extended morning session, but Kelsey had thought it was a positive sign. Brandon clearly wasn't about to let his injuries keep him down for long.

"Grueling. It's discouraging to see how out of shape you can get in a couple of weeks."

Out of shape? Kelsey stole another glance in his direction. He sat with one arm over the back of the seat, his fingers resting just an inch from her shoulders. At that angle, his long-sleeved shirt pulled slightly against his chest, hinting at the firm molding of muscles underneath. He was thin, maybe, but out of shape? Not a bit.

She held her breath, remembering those hard muscles beneath her hands. It was such a strange feeling, knowing an intimate secret about him, which gave her the power to see right through the civilized veneer of shirt and slacks and smile.

She flexed her tense, moist fingers. She knew that, under the shirt, his skin was golden, like honey in the sun. She knew it was as smooth to the touch as polished satinwood. She knew it was warm and pulsing and alive.

And he didn't know that she knew.

"It'll come back to you quickly," she said, then flushed at her choice of words: he might think she was talking about his memory. "Your getting in shape, I mean."

One corner of his mouth tucked into his cheek. "Tea leaves again?" he asked, but this time his tone was only mildly sarcastic. "Or are you always such a cockeyed optimist?"

"Neither," she said carefully, determined that this conversation, at least, would not degenerate into an argument. "I simply have a lot of faith in you."

Her answer seemed to startle him. His head jerked toward her slightly, though he immediately checked the motion, and the wry smile died from his lips. For a minute he didn't speak, his body tense and his head tilted, as if he was trying to dissect and analyze her surprising words.

In the end, he seemed to choose to ignore them, as if they were some strange object he needed to set aside for further examination later. She saw him shrug away the tension and take a deep breath.

"I guess I've always taken my body for granted," he said, harking back to the original subject as if she hadn't spoken. "There's something about tramping twenty miles in the jungle or trotting up a hundred stairs to the top of a Mayan temple. It's better than any treadmill for keeping you huffing and puffing."

"I can imagine," she said, pleased that he had introduced this new topic. Surely, if she could get him to talk about archaeology, the trip into San Francisco would pass smoothly.

She loved to hear him talk about his work. Often, when Douglas used to go out to dinner meetings, Brandon and Ginny would join her in the office just before Ginny's bedtime and the three of them would chat companionably about Brandon's exotic experiences while Kelsey filed furniture estimates or compared computer prices. She'd always enjoyed those lazy, low-key visits, and had loved his descriptions of the wet, green jungles and the magnificent, crumbling temples just as much as Ginny did.

Back then it had been a welcome escape from Douglas's world of petty power to Brandon's bigger world, where a sense of history put individual problems into truer perspective. It was an escape now, too. Thousand-year-old tragedies were safely remote and dusty, the tears long dried, the pain long past.

Brandon seemed glad of the diversion, as well. She asked a couple of questions, and he told an amusing story about a mischievous visiting professor who confounded his students by asking them to identify an "artifact" that turned out to be a clay pencil-holder his preschooler had made for

Father's Day. They both laughed as Brandon recounted the wild theories the desperate students had come up with, and gradually Kelsey's fingers loosened their aching grip on the wheel.

Before it seemed possible, they were at the outskirts of the city.

"Which exit should I take?" She didn't know whether Mr. Fuller was another archaeologist or an ODC connection, although, since his name wasn't at all familiar, she tended toward the former. "We're just north of town right now. Where is Mr. Fuller's office?"

He seemed strangely reluctant to focus on Mr. Fuller. "It's downtown," he said vaguely. "But my appointment's not until five. We have to eat first. Why don't we go to the Wharf?"

"The Wharf?" She was surprised, and she sounded it. She had been wondering where he'd feel comfortable eating. At home he ate alone, seeming to dislike being watched while he struggled with the food. She'd thought he'd suggest somewhere expensive and sedate, where the stuffy dignity of the waiters and other customers would guarantee no gawking sympathy. Or maybe even a fast-food place where a burger could be ordered at the drive-through and eaten in the privacy of the car. "Fisherman's Wharf?"

"Yeah," he said. "There's a great little Chinese restaurant at the end of the pier. I can't handle chopsticks just yet, I guess, but I'll bet I can manage to eat a couple of egg rolls without disgracing myself."

"But, Brandon..." She didn't know quite what to say. It had been so wonderful to spend this pleasant time with him, and she didn't want anything to ruin it. She was afraid that the strain of maneuvering the Wharf would upset him, would bring back all the pain and frustration, and with it the angry Brandon who seemed to resent her so bitterly. "It'll be such a long walk. And it'll be so crowded..."

"I'll manage. You can hold my hand and keep me from falling into the bay," he said, his tone flippant. But then, as if sensing her concern, he turned toward her, and his voice grew serious. "Listen, Kelsey, I *want* a crowd. I've been going crazy this past week, with that horrible hospital room and that damn house where everyone tiptoes around. I need to get out. I need to smell the salt air and hear people shouting and laughing."

"But your leg..." She could hardly believe he meant it, but longing was powerful in his voice. "Won't it hurt to walk so far?"

"It'll be good for me. Pain builds character."

"Brandon—"

"Let's go, Kelsey. It'll be fun. You're not ashamed of me, are you? I promise not to dribble my tea, and besides, everyone at the Wharf is a tourist. No one you know will see you there having lunch with a pitiful blind guy."

"Brandon!" She touched his hand angrily. "That's ridiculous, and you know it!"

He grabbed her hand and held it. "Yes, I do know it." He smiled, and the sight of that smile, so familiar, so like her Brandon, sent tears rushing to her eyes. "Come on. Let's do it. It's been a tough time for both of us, and I know I've been hard to live with. Let's put that behind us for a couple of hours. I may not remember everything, but I do remember that we used to have fun together. Didn't we?"

Not trusting her voice, she nodded, trying vainly to hold back the tears.

But he couldn't see her. "Didn't we?" he asked again, squeezing her hand to corral her attention.

"Yes," she somehow managed to say, "we did."

They ate at an outside table, the warmth of the noonday sun offsetting the cold breeze that blew across the bay. Gulls rode the wind, cawing in high, excited voices, and the long dock below them teemed with unwieldy sea lions who barked incessantly as they tumbled over one another. Brandon cocked his head toward the cacophony and laughed.

"It's funny," he said. "When you can't see what they are, they sound like a clown convention, all honking their horns at the same time."

Closing her eyes, Kelsey listened and began to chuckle. He was right. In the past when she'd heard the sea lions she'd thought the sound mournful, but she knew it would never seem so to her again. She would always think of clowns, and it would make her smile.

So why, once again, did tears sting her eyes even while she laughed? She watched him as he sat across from her, the sun winking through his fair hair as the wind ruffled it away from his bandages. Perhaps it was because his reaction to the sea lions was the essence of his magic. He loved life, every foolish, glorious minute of it. Where others found melancholy, he found laughter. And when you were with him, you saw the world as he did. It seemed a much grander place.

They were still sitting quietly, listening to the unique bustle of the Wharf, when the waitress came for their order. Brandon requested his egg rolls without a trace of self-consciousness, looking anything but pitiful. In fact, two women at the next table took in every inch of him, from his gleaming hair to the long, muscular leg he kept stretched out slightly to one side.

Absurdly, Kelsey found herself prickling with resentment. She caught the gaze of one of the women, and then, with deliberate emphasis, she reached out to adjust the crutch that rested against the table.

Her fingers lingered on the cushion at the top, which was still warm from being tucked under Brandon's arm. It was a decidedly proprietary gesture, and she was pleased to see the acquisitive light fade from the woman's eye as she processed Kelsey's message. *The crutch, and the man who uses it,* the gesture said, *are mine.*

But a minute later, Kelsey let go of the crutch, suddenly feeling like an idiot. What kind of primitive instincts were these? Why shouldn't the women admire him? Kelsey didn't *own* him—far from it.

She was letting herself be deceived by the artificial intimacy created when they'd walked slowly down the pier to the restaurant, arms linked, bodies pressed close together from hip to shoulder so that Brandon could follow her movements safely.

They had worked well together, finding their rhythm quickly, communicating physically with amazing ease. There was something quite sensual about it. They didn't talk, concentrating on each nuance of muscle movements, attuned to tiny shifts of pace or direction. With each step Kelsey's body seemed to mold itself more closely to Brandon's, until she wasn't sure where she ended and he began.

The walk had probably seemed like an endless labor of pain to him, but she had selfishly wished the pier would stretch out magically before them, never coming to an end, never reaching the point at which they must separate and become, once again, two people.

"I thought you were a cashew-chicken kind of lady."

"Hmm?" Kelsey started at the sound of Brandon's voice.

"Oh, yes, that's right," she said, shaking off the remembered feel of his body and making sense of his words. Often, on her late nights, she'd order Chinese food to eat in the office. She remembered how Brandon, perched on the edge of the desk, would rummage through the cardboard box with her chopsticks, searching for the last delicious cashews. She'd bat his hand away without taking her eyes from the computer.

He obviously remembered, too. He remembered everything about her, didn't he? Every *trivial* thing, everything that didn't matter.

"Well, I usually am, but I'm in the mood for egg rolls today," she lied. She hated egg rolls, but she couldn't bring herself to order anything he couldn't have.

"That really isn't necessary," he said quietly, putting his hand on the table between them. "But it's very sweet."

As she looked at his strong hand, so golden against the white tablecloth, her fingers itched to reach out and touch it. Perhaps, she encouraged herself, he was hoping she would. He couldn't grab hold of her hand as he might once have done, so maybe he was asking her to take the initiative.

But his palm was facedown, not up, which would have been a more direct request. She knit her fingers together, her pulse throbbing where they pressed too tightly. Suppose she was misinterpreting the gesture? Suppose he twitched away from her the way he had in the hospital? Fear trapped her in a sludge of doubt, and her hands remained locked in her lap.

In a minute he withdrew his hand without comment. "And it's really too bad," he added in a more normal voice. "This is probably the one time your cashews would have been safe from me."

She stared at the empty tablecloth. "I should have thought of that," she said, striving for a light tone even though she felt glum, as if she'd just missed a chance for something very special. She was glad he couldn't see her face.

"Take advantage while you can," he said, his tone teasing. "When these bandages come off it's every nut for himself."

She tried to put a smile in her voice, tried to screen any hint of doubt. They both knew what might happen when the bandages came off. "I'll bet you can hardly wait."

"Well, I've tried everything I can think of to get James to take them off sooner, but he's a bullheaded old cuss and he just told me to learn some patience." Brandon laughed and, carefully feeling for his glass, took a drink of water. "He still thinks I'm only ten, hiding an ice cube in my mouth while he took my temperature so he'd let me play in the big baseball game."

A smile tugged Kelsey's lips. "Did you really do that?"

"That's what they tell me. All I remember is that I hit one over the fence and then passed out at home plate." He looked sheepish, but boyishly triumphant. "A hundred and five by the clinic thermometer. But we won."

"Good heavens!" Kelsey shook her head in dismay. "Ginny seems to have inherited the same competitive streak."

Brandon smiled, toying with the glass he still held. "Yeah. We're a lot alike, I think. Douglas always says we—"

He broke off midsentence. His face paled, and he clenched his water glass so tightly his fingernails went completely white.

Kelsey didn't know what to say. More accurately, she knew there was nothing she *could* say. And yet her mind kept trying, kept sorting through all the polite phrases of sympathy, entreaty and reassurance, looking for the magic one that would take the strain from his features.

But if such a phrase existed, she couldn't utter it. He'd told her never to mention Douglas to him again. She held her breath and waited.

"I'm sorry," he said, letting go of the glass and running his hand through his hair. "I still can't believe it."

"I know," she began, but at that moment the waitress appeared again, carrying two cups of egg drop soup, which apparently came with the meal they'd ordered. Kelsey sat in quiet consternation as the young woman put a cup in front of each of them, wondering whether she should signal her to take it away. He couldn't handle soup.

But it was already too late. "Smells good," Brandon said, smiling up toward the waitress, who looked quite smug, as if she had whipped up some exotic delicacy all by herself and presented it to him. Her self-satisfied expression made Kelsey feel disproportionately grumpy. It was just soup, for heaven's sake, not the milk of paradise! Couldn't she tell how difficult it would be for him to eat it?

But when the waitress retreated, and Brandon turned his smile toward Kelsey, her ill temper disappeared like a rabbit under a magician's wand. "Go ahead," he said. "Eat it while it's warm."

She hesitated. "I'm not terribly hungry," she said, dipping her spoon into the soup and stirring the white specks around aimlessly.

"No? Well, *I* am." She looked up, frowning. How would he manage?

He might have read her mind. "You'll have to help me," he said with a half smile, and her hand stilled on the spoon, which had grown uncomfortably hot under her fingers.

Help him? "How?" Her voice was almost a squeak.

"Like this." He extended his arm and with unconscious grace felt for her hand. She watched as he came closer, so close she felt his warmth emanating onto her tingling skin.

She didn't reach out to guide him. He would find her; she knew it.

And he did. He touched first the soft nook of her elbow and let his fingers wrap slowly around it, as if learning the shape of her in this new and completely tactile way. Then he ran the tips of his fingers along her inner arm and settled over the hand that held the burning spoon.

Her heart tripped, and she stared mutely at their joined hands, like subtle layers of gold, dark over pale, rough over smooth. When she didn't respond, he nudged with his first two fingers, urging her to move the spoon.

"Like this," he repeated, and her hand obeyed, scooping the liquid into the bowl of the spoon. And then, still hand in hand, he guided it toward his mouth.

She watched, transfixed, never thinking to take her hand away, feeling the small constriction of muscle as he swallowed. Then he pulled the spoon slowly from his lips. "Like that," he said, his voice thickened, and suddenly her heart was beating wildly in her throat. Perhaps it was the milk of paradise, after all.

And already he was guiding her back again, urging her toward the steaming cup. But as they neared it, she pulled her hand away, and the spoon clattered onto the table.

He tilted his head and didn't try to retrieve the spoon.

"Is that all, Kelsey?" His voice was still husky. "One taste and no more?"

"I . . ." Released from his touch, she felt her heart begin to settle its pace. Common sense was returning, and with it another tweak of embarrassment. Nothing had really happened here—except in her own overstimulated imagination. She'd helped him with the soup, just as Frances or Ginny or the nurse in the hospital had probably done. That was all.

But if that really was all, why did she feel so emotionally wrung out?

"I thought you didn't like egg drop soup," she finished lamely. Whether or not it was all in her imagination, she only knew she couldn't feed him another spoonful.

"I don't think I ever said that. I may have said it wasn't good for me. Or maybe—" his voice lowered "—I said I shouldn't allow myself to indulge in too much of it." He circled his finger along the rim of his own cup, barely avoiding touching the wetness within. "But I don't think I ever said I didn't like it."

She looked at him. Was he toying with her—or was this another overheated fantasy? She frowned, unsure. If only she could see his eyes. She needed them to act as her interpreter. But the white bandages stared blankly at her, foiling any attempt to decipher his ambiguous words.

"Maybe," she said, with a touch of ice in the word. If there *was* a double meaning here, she had one to offer of her own. "Or maybe you've just forgotten whether you liked it or not."

CHAPTER NINE

AL FULLER'S OFFICE reeked of money. Brandon didn't need to see a single piece of furniture to know that this was no ratty private eye's lair, the kind in an old Humphrey Bogart movie. The air was luxuriously chilly and scented with the delicate aroma of the fresh flowers near the receptionist's desk and the subtle odor of real leather coming from the roomy wing chair he sat in now.

But he hated the place just the same. He didn't want to be here. He wanted to be back at the Wharf with Kelsey, letting her spoon-feed him egg drop soup, which he didn't even like.

Strange. Incredible, really. He couldn't think of another human being he would have allowed to feed him. He would have starved first. But with Kelsey everything was different.

Take the way he'd felt when she led him down the pier. He hadn't been afraid or self-conscious. It felt so good, so *right*, to have her next to him, pressing close.

That was natural. Blind or not, he was still a man, and any man would welcome the feel of Kelsey Whittaker's body against his. But it was more than that. He trusted her. Trust. It sounded like a simple word, but it wasn't. When the nurse, or Greg, or even Frances helped him get around, he was always on his guard, ultracareful, his internal radar scanning constantly, his reflexes on alert, never depending fully on anyone else to protect and guide him.

With Kelsey, he had been able to abandon that exhausting struggle for control. He hadn't thought about the hundreds of people milling around them, hadn't racked his brain to remember how often the pier had stairs, hadn't worried about the meaning of every flickering shadow his bandages let through. That was trust to a degree he'd never experienced before. That was trust he hadn't known was possible.

It utterly confused him. Why, on this profound, subconscious level, should he trust a woman his conscious mind suspected of all kinds of ugly things? How could he feel this faith in her when he knew she had, at the very least, callously toyed with Douglas's heart and, at the most, tormented him straight to his death? When he feared that the Traherne bank account had been her only reason for wearing Douglas's ring? She'd admitted that her father gambled. . . .

"Hello, Mr. Traherne." Fuller's oily voice was right beside him, and Brandon tried not to recoil. The private detective patted his shoulder rather than attempt a handshake, and for that, Brandon was grateful. Trying to locate Fuller's hand would have felt like a Three Stooges routine, and he'd been dreading it. "Sorry to keep you waiting."

"We'll have to make this short. Kelsey will be driving me home, and I hate to ask her to wait out there too long."

"Yes, I saw Miss Whittaker in the lobby," Fuller said, and somehow Brandon knew the investigator was smiling. Brandon also knew it wasn't a kind smile. "Beautiful woman, isn't she? Almost too good-looking for comfort, I used to tell your brother. Remember the old song—if you want to be happy, marry an ugly girl?" Fuller laughed, and the sound was not quite as classy as the office. "Of course, I would have lost a bundle in surveillance fees if Douglas had taken that advice."

Brandon found himself making a fist with his right hand and forced his fingers to relax. God, how had Douglas stood this toad? "You said you had an urgent report for me?"

"Right." Brandon heard the rustle of papers with a sinking heart. Fuller's comments had confirmed his fears—the report must be about Kelsey. He thought piercingly of her warm body next to his, leading him safely down the pier, and yet he knew he couldn't stop himself from listening to whatever Fuller said. He had to find out which was right, his primitive instinct to trust or his conscious deductions, which warned him to doubt.

"Let's see." More rustling as Fuller scanned the report. "Well, we can skip the preliminary setup. Let's just cut to the chase." He made a smug tsking sound. "Hmm, it seems your Mr. Farnham isn't quite the wholesome American father figure his advertising would suggest."

Brandon started. "Farnham?"

"Yes, of course. You know, 'Farnham Foods—Your Family's Friend' and all that? Well, it seems Mr. Farnham, who's fifty-three, has a taste for twenty-year-old bimbos. We didn't find any real dirt unfortunately—no paternity suits, no abortions, no married women or suicidal ex-wives—but I still think there's something in here you can use."

Brandon's blood pounded. *"Use?"* he said ominously.

"Yeah, I really think so." Fuller didn't seem to sense anything amiss. He rustled some more papers. "I think you can suggest that you're taking a risk getting involved with a company that is so ripe for scandal. He'll know it's not true—no exposure for you, of course—but he'll be put on notice that you know about his little habits. He'll be a lot less likely to play hardball."

So many unmanageable emotions were flooding through Brandon's mind—a hot desire to grab Fuller by the tie to stop the flow of smarmy words, sickening disgust that Douglas should have struck up a partnership with such a man, burning shame that he had come to this appointment in the first place and a swamping relief that the report hadn't been about Kelsey. For a moment he simply sat paralyzed, unable to react in any way.

"I can read you the whole report if you like, but that's the gist of it." Fuller tapped the pages on the desktop, organizing them into a pile and obviously feeling self-satisfied. "Your final meeting with Farnham is tomorrow, isn't it? You can see, I'm sure, why I thought you needed to hear the report today."

"No," Brandon said, forcing the word through iron lips. "No, I can't. Frankly, I can't imagine what the hell was going through my brother's mind to commission such a report. I want you to burn it. And if he commissioned others, burn them, too."

There was a shocked silence, in which even the paper tapping stopped. Fuller cleared his throat. "*If* there were others? Mr. Traherne, your brother got a report just like this on every client he had. And on every employee in his company, right down to the janitors. Perhaps after all these years out digging in the jungle you don't realize it, but for many companies this is standard business practice."

"I don't give a damn. It's outrageous. Burn them."

"He also asked for one on every teacher at your sister's school." Fuller sounded frigid, and Brandon knew he had deeply insulted the man. "And every neighbor in a three-mile radius."

"Burn them, damn it."

"And, I might add," Fuller went on, his tone deceptively cool and bland, "on every girl you've so much as flirted with since you were nineteen years old. Up to and including the delectable Kelsey Whittaker."

Brandon fought back a shockingly physical wave of nausea and stood up, unable to control the tension in his muscles. Adrenaline shot through his bloodstream, demanding action. Fight or flight. Oh, God, if only it could be fight! If only he could see to squash this slimy insect!

He got to his feet. "Burn them," he said again, his voice venomous. "No. I don't trust you to do it. Give them to me, and I'll burn them."

He heard the slow scraping as Fuller pushed his chair back and stood up, too. He knew they were facing off, in the classic pose of mortal confrontation. "Well, I'm not sure I can do that, Mr. Traherne." The oil was back in his voice, but it didn't hide the fury the man clearly felt. "Those documents belonged to your brother, and I need legal permission to turn them over to anyone, including you."

Brandon moved around the chair and gripped its high back so hard his hands ached. Until he realized Brandon didn't approve, Fuller had been perfectly willing to share every juicy morsel of gossip he had, like two rats over a carcass.

But why try to argue with him? The man was slippery by profession and venal by nature, and every word out of his mouth would just be a lie.

"Fine," Brandon said coldly. "In the meantime, you just make damn sure no one else sees those things."

"Oh, I see what's really bothering you, Mr. Traherne." Now Fuller was laughing at him under the oil, and Brandon was glad the chair and desk stood between them. "But you needn't worry. We never found anything very damaging about you and Miss Whittaker, just a lot of mooning glances and a couple of late nights in the office getting cozy over the computer. And, of course, one or two sophomoric touchy-feely episodes like that accidentally-on-purpose tackle in the flower bed."

"Why, you bast—"

"Oh, don't worry," Fuller repeated tauntingly. "Douglas didn't mind. He thought it was funny. He knew you didn't have a chance. Miss Whittaker was after bigger fish than you."

Red flashes went off behind Brandon's eyes as he fumbled for his crutch. He had to get out of this room immediately. Blind or not blind, he might kill the man if he stayed.

"You'll get a fax from my lawyer by eleven o'clock tomorrow," he said through clenched teeth, as he limped painfully toward what he hoped was the door. "And those reports had better be on my desk by noon."

"WAIT. LET'S NOT GO into the house just yet."

After the long, silent trip home, the sound of Brandon's voice was almost startling. Kelsey stopped abruptly a few yards from the front door and stared at him as if he had just performed a magic trick. Though she hadn't dared to voice it, she hadn't wanted to go in yet, either.

She wanted the day to last longer, but Brandon had seemed so preoccupied that she hadn't guessed he felt the same way. When he had come barreling out of Fuller's office, he had been on fire with an inarticulate rage. She'd rushed to his side to steer him through the maze of lobby furniture, and his skin had felt feverish under her fingers.

She couldn't imagine what had put him into such a fury. She didn't even know what kind of business Mr. Fuller was in. The office was discreetly anonymous; the nameplate offered no explanations. She could tell it wasn't a doctor's office—which was a relief—but Mr. Fuller could have been a lawyer or an investment counselor or a voodoo priest, for all she knew.

But whoever the mysterious Mr. Fuller was, he'd managed to make Brandon angrier than she'd ever seen him. Too angry, apparently, even to talk about it. After venturing a few tentative questions that received only clipped answers, she had subsided, concentrating on driving.

Only as the car cleared the congested freeway had he begun to calm down.

"Sorry to be such poor company," he'd said at one point. "It was a rather grim meeting."

"That's okay," she'd responded quietly, because it was. It sounded corny, but she was content just to be with him, silent or chatty, safe in this glassed-in privacy, speeding past the fretful world. She wanted the drive to go on forever.

But, of course, it didn't. Dusk had already fallen by the time their own little mountain came into sight, twinkling with lights, as if the sky had rained stars. With an inner sigh, she turned onto Cliff Road and began the climb toward the highest star, which she knew was the light from Brandon's tower bedroom.

She'd been resigned to seeing their day together end, but now he was giving her this unexpected reprieve. Joy grabbed her throat, and she couldn't speak for a moment.

"All right. What do you want to do?" she said at last.

"Mind if we just sit in the garden?" He still had her arm tucked under his elbow, which had seemed to work the best while she was helping him walk. "Just for a little while."

Mind? "Sounds great," she said, and they turned away from the house toward the garden, which overlooked the bay. She could see the water from here, rippling and gleaming under the starlight. "It's a beautiful night."

Brandon knew every inch of this property by heart. His pace was quicker and surer than it had been on the pier, his dependence on her less complete. She should have been glad for him—*was* glad for him—but selfishly she missed the intimacy that dependence had required. All too soon they stood beside the iron benches that overlooked the bay, and he let go of her arm.

"It smells like a good night," he said, breathing in the cool, clean air deeply as he sank onto the bench, propping the crutch beside him. "Sit down, Kelsey, and tell me about it."

Joining him, she gazed upward. "Well, it's clear," she said, wondering if that was what he meant. "The sky is very black—there's just a fingernail moon—but there are a million stars. They seem close enough to touch."

He made a low murmur of appreciation. "You know," he said, "you never see that kind of sky in the jungle. The trees are too tall, too thick. It's like being inside a dark, wet cocoon. But in its own way, it's beautiful, too."

"Yes," she said, trying to imagine a world where you couldn't see the stars. "It must be."

And then they sat in silence. He tilted his head back, presenting his face to the starshine as if he could feel it glittering down on him, and she watched his clean, proud profile, memorizing every detail.

After a minute he sighed and lowered his head.

"James takes these blasted things off tomorrow," he said, touching his bandages. Yes, she thought, in this condition, he would find mountain nights and jungle nights sadly the same.

"I know," she said. "I know you'll be glad."

"God, yes!" His voice was fervent, almost a whisper. And then, abruptly, he turned his face to her and said, as if on an impulse too fierce to resist, "Come out here with me tomorrow night, so that we can see the stars together."

Stunned, she looked at him. Just like the old Brandon, he sounded confident that he'd be able to see when the bandages were removed. And, in the face of his groundless certainty, her own paradoxically faded. So many things could still go wrong.

He kept his face turned toward her, waiting for her answer. Starlight silvered his fair hair, painting the bandages a stark and eerie white, and she was strangely reminded of a blindfolded prisoner, facing his enemies with a doomed dignity.

The image took her breath away. With a sudden surge of panic, she found she couldn't speak.

"Kelsey?" He stretched his hand along the back of the bench until his fingers touched her upper arm.

Her hair, which she had worn loose today, tumbled over her shoulders, and finding it, he slid his fingers into its heavy thickness. He touched only the last, curving inches of hair, but her scalp tingled as the strands shifted, transmitting the sensations clearly to every nerve ending. "Your hair is very dark," he said, once again changing the subject. Slowly he rubbed a lock of it back and forth between his fingers. "As dark as coffee. The sun can make it look a little lighter, but when it's wet it's almost black. And tonight . . ."

He twisted his hand, draping the hair under his thumb and wrapping it like a rope around his knuckles. Though her hair was long, the motion tugged her head an inch closer to his. "Tonight," he said, his voice low, "under so many stars, it must be glowing like polished mahogany."

Coffee, mahogany—hardly the most flowery words in the world, and yet something in his tone made them sound like poetry. Kelsey shivered, a tiny ripple that started deep and shimmered out into her limbs.

"I think your memory is flattering me," she said, and her voice vibrated slightly, the shiver affecting it like a soft breeze over water. "It's really just a mousy brown."

"No." He shook his head. "I'm not imagining it. I remember how beautiful you are. I even remember . . ." He paused, stroking his thumb over the captured ribbon of hair. "Even before I touched it, I knew how thick and silky it would be, how it would feel like water spilling over my skin."

He knew. Her heart was barely beating; her lungs had to be reminded to breathe. Of course he knew. She stared down at his hand, tangled in the glossy strands, and she was afraid to say anything.

He was remembering. The words fluttered through her like stardust. He was remembering.

"I've had such thoughts, Kelsey. Clear. And so real they hurt. From the first day we met, I've thought about how beautiful you are. I've thought about—" he halted again and took a deep breath "—everything. I knew I had no right, but I couldn't stop myself. The fantasies were so deeply imbedded that I couldn't burn them out."

Still she dared not speak, for fear she would, by placing herself in its path, somehow divert the flow of memory. *Let it become a flood,* she prayed, *until he remembers everything.*

He opened his hand, letting the hair trickle through his fingers. His head was tilted at a slight angle, suggesting a bemusement that was reflected in his voice.

"It's ironic, isn't it? The thoughts are still there—in spite of all that's happened. That accident blew my life to bits, but it couldn't blast me free from those fantasies. They're still as sharp, as tormentingly real, as ever. I still think about how you would feel in my arms, how your lips would taste, how your body would tremble when I—"

A small cry escaped her lips before she could bite it back, and her hand, almost of its own volition, came to rest on his knee.

"Brandon," she said, wanting to tell him his fantasies were more, so much more, than that, but the one word was all she could manage.

"I knew you'd say my name like that." He lowered his head and, turning her palm up, he began a slow massage with his thumb. First he traced the sensitive ridges in her hand, like a fortune-teller reading her palm. Her skin caught fire, and the fire slid silently through her veins to the rest of her body. "Strange how vivid imagination can be. I *knew* that when you wanted me to touch you, your voice would sound just like that."

"Yes," she said, as if he'd asked her a question. His thumb had worked its way to her wrist, where her pulse throbbed against the pressure, shooting tingling sparks up her arm and into her chest.

"Oh, Brandon, what..." she began, but she felt a sudden breathlessness, and the end of her sentence became merely a frantic gasp of air.

His fingers closed around her wrist like a silken handcuff.

"What I want," he said, his head still bent over her hand, "is for you to kiss me."

Kiss him. As he lifted his head slowly, she stared helplessly at his mouth, at those firm, curving lips that were made for laughter. They were made for love, too, and the memory made her heart begin a primitive beat.

She knew those lips. Wide and generous lips, but also tight and strong, with a hard outline that made them intoxicatingly masculine. When they touched her, wherever they touched her, they felt like no other lips she'd ever known.

Would he remember her lips? If she kissed him now, would it, like the fairy-tale kiss, awaken his slumbering memories? Would the fantasy finally show itself to be truth?

He waited, starlight rimming with silver the strong, ridged bow of the upper lip, pooling on the sensual pout of the lower. Then, as he let his lips part slightly, it glinted off a hint of white teeth, teasing her, before disappearing.

Kelsey felt suddenly boneless, as if she was made of nothing but naked emotions and exposed nerve endings. Kiss him . . .

"Kiss me, Kelsey." It was an order, a velvet-covered command, issued from deep in his throat, in a wizard's hypnotic tones. He didn't shift a millimeter in her direction—he knew he didn't have to. He would not fumble, groping for her face, feeling for her lips. He would simply wait, and she would bring the kiss to him.

Slowly, as if she were a vessel filled to overflowing, she leaned toward him, trying to keep the motion steady, trying to prevent the intense, liquid desire she felt from pouring out of her. Just a drop, just one warm drop of love. One kiss, one gentle kiss on those waiting, starlit lips.

And for one suspended moment he let it be that way. Without making a single movement of his own, he let her brush her lips across his, warmth to warmth, anointing him with the soft touch. She shut her eyes, holding back, trying to contain the rest. . . .

But when she began to pull away, everything changed. He transformed, in one skipped heartbeat, from quiescent recipient to master. With a low groan, he took her head in both hands and pulled her into him, rocking her off balance, forcing her to spill the entire, flooding truth of her need against his parted lips.

As if even that couldn't satisfy him, he pressed harder, bruising her, searching for anything she might be holding back. She moaned into his opened mouth, and his hands tunneled into her hair, his fingers closing over the crown of her head with a triumph of possession. His tongue drove into her like a flame, demanding that she acknowledge herself his prisoner.

All resistance blew away like smoke. She sagged against him, surrendering to the sweet fire, knowing how it would burn, yet somehow bewitched beyond caring. What more could she want than to be prisoner of the man she loved, to answer his flame with flame of her own? He would be her prisoner, too. There came a time, in such a burning, when both were equally consumed....

"Well, this is a pretty picture, I must say."

At the incredible, impossible sound of her father's voice—and yet it *was* her father—Kelsey pulled herself violently from Brandon's arms, like a terrified teenager.

"Dad!" At her side, Brandon had gone rigid, she noticed with the small fraction of her mind that was still functioning. She couldn't label the emotion that held him in such motionless thrall. Embarrassment, anger, frustration—none of them quite fit the controlled tension that emanated from him now. She swallowed and tried to quiet her heartbeat. "What are you doing here?"

"I love you, too, sweetheart," Tim Whittaker said, affecting a wounded air. In spite of her own pounding confusion, Kelsey spotted right away that the "s" of "sweetheart" dragged a little. She'd had long years of practice spotting such things.

Her father had been drinking. After two weeks of sobriety, during which she'd allowed herself to hope the shock of Douglas's death had forced him into recovery, he was as drunk as ever. She fought back defeated tears and tried to think. If only she could get him away. If only Brandon wouldn't notice.

"Here I come to visit my best girl, and this is the welcome I get?" Her father was pouting now.

"You should have called," she said through stiff lips that still felt swollen. Pity notwithstanding, she was furious with him, and not just because he'd picked such a miserable moment to arrive. She knew that wheedling tone. He wanted something.

And then she realized what must have brought on the binge. He'd been gambling again and, as ever, he'd lost. So here he was, wanting what he always wanted—money. She could only hope he'd wait until they were alone to discuss it.

But her father was chuckling, a knowing grin on his impish features. His cheeks were bright pink, even in the starlight. "Should have called!" He laughed as if it was a very funny joke. "Yes, I see that. Bit of bad timing, hmm? But, honestly, sweetheart, I'm glad I happened in when I did. It's good to know you and Brandon are . . . such good friends. I'm needing a little help, you see, and your friend Brandon may be able to help me better than you can, sweetheart."

"Dad," she said with all the quelling intensity she could muster. "*Dad.*" She stood up, though her legs were still warm and weak. "Maybe we should talk inside. Alone."

"I don't know, sweetheart." Her father shook his head. "I'm afraid the trouble I'm in is deeper than *your* pockets."

"That's enough, Dad," she said firmly, horrified at how blatant he was daring to be. He must have read a great deal more into the kiss he witnessed than she realized. Did he really think they could bleed first one brother and then the other? Suddenly her anger and disgust outweighed her pity. "Let's go. We don't want to bore Brandon with all this."

"Nonsense." With a stern authority, Brandon stood up and reached for his crutch. "I'm not a bit bored." He took one limping step forward and held out his arm. "Let's go in to the office, and your father can tell us both what's the matter."

Kelsey looked from one man to the other with a sense of despair. Brandon's mouth was firm; clearly he was determined to hear her father out. Her father, on the other hand, was smiling.

"Come on, then," he said, grabbing her hand and slapping it over Brandon's elbow. "The man wants to help. The least you can do is give him a hand."

CHAPTER TEN

BY THE TIME he got to the end of his tale, Tim Whittaker had sobered up significantly. Kelsey sat at his side, holding his hand, feeling as if she were underwater, hearing and seeing everything through a dense opacity.

She'd argued all the way up to Brandon's office, trying to make her father see that they should not air this new difficulty in front of Brandon. But her father, who obviously sensed that Brandon might be persuaded to help, was determined to talk, and Brandon, for his own dark reasons, was determined to hear.

She'd almost refused to join them, hoping that would show Brandon, at least, that she would not be a part of this . . . this panhandling. But fear of what her father might say, without her there to muzzle him, kept her chained to the room.

Throughout the recitation Brandon had been silent. He sat behind his desk looking, Kelsey thought, ironically like blind Justice, not seeing her father's shame or her own embarrassment—just dispassionately weighing the facts.

It was the same old story. A bookie had offered Tim good odds, and he hadn't been able to resist.

"How much did you lose?"

Kelsey and her father glanced up simultaneously at Brandon's calm question. The resemblance to Justice no longer seemed to fit at all. Had Justice's lips ever worn such a subtle curl of cynicism? Brandon didn't look shocked by her father's revelations. He looked like a man whose lowest opinion of human nature had just been confirmed. She turned her head away.

"How much?"

"Five thousand dollars," her father answered, and he had the grace to flush slightly.

Kelsey groaned. She hadn't expected it to be so high. "Oh, Dad," she whispered, pressing her fingers into her eyes until they hurt, as if she could make the whole mortifying scene disappear. "Dad, how could you?"

"He was offering me five to one." Her father's voice was bleakly regretful. "If I'd won, it would have paid twenty-five thousand. You know what that would have meant to us, Kelsey."

Of course she knew. "But you didn't win," she said in a low voice, not looking at him. "You never do."

Her father pulled his hand away. "I used to," he said simply, but the three words spoke volumes. Her heart pinching, Kelsey glanced at Brandon, wondering if he could hear the insecurity and battered self-esteem behind those little words.

"Dad," she broke in wretchedly. "*Please* don't drag Brandon into this. Come to my room. We'll think of something—"

"I used to win. I put you through college on it," he went on, seeming not to hear her. "It wasn't a fancy college, not the kind you really deserved, but..." Her father's eyes were red and glistening, and her soul sank. So it was going to be *that* kind of night, the kind that was marshy with tears and self-pity. Well, perhaps that was better than the other kind, in which her father was bloated with ranting bravado.

"Oh, Dad, I know what you did for me," she said, and her gratitude was not feigned. He had helped, though the tiny check that sometimes came and more often didn't had just barely covered the cost of textbooks. Still, she knew how hard it was for him to save even that much, and cherishing the love it represented, she took out college loans, and got evening jobs typing dissertations and weekend jobs waiting tables, anything she could find.

But clearly he wanted to look good in Brandon's eyes, and, as always, she allowed him the small charade.

Brandon broke in coldly, apparently unmoved. "Let me see if I understand this. Are you asking Kelsey to settle this debt?"

Her father wriggled uncomfortably. "Well, there's nothing I hate more than bringing problems here to Kelsey, but—"

"But you're doing it, anyway." Brandon's voice was grim.

"Where else can I turn?" Her father's eyes were still shining, and Kelsey's heart twisted. She hated to see him this way. Even worse, she hated for Brandon to think that this was the sum total of Tim Whittaker—a maudlin, weak-willed drunk.

No man should be judged by his weaknesses alone. She lifted her chin, though Brandon couldn't see her.

Brandon knew nothing about the years her father had raised her by himself, the nights he'd paced the floor, singing Irish lullabies while he guarded her through a high fever. Brandon couldn't know about the hours her father had taken off, without pay, to watch her win the oration contest or to stand, red-faced and stoic, near the dressing room as she tried on prom dresses.

And Brandon couldn't imagine how hard her father tried to stay sober or how he hated himself when he failed.

She took her father's hand again and looked steadily toward Brandon. "I *want* him to come to me," she said firmly. "I wouldn't want him to go to anyone else." She stressed the last, and hoped that Brandon would read her meaning.

"Where else can I go?" her father said. "Who else is there?"

Brandon cocked his head. "Now that my brother is dead, you mean?"

It was his tone as much as his words that carried the insult, and Kelsey's head snapped back fractionally, as if she'd been slapped. Her father was slower to understand, slower to react, but within a few seconds a red burn rose slowly up the thick column of his neck and into his cheeks.

"I'm not sure what you mean," her father said stiffly.

"Douglas paid your father's debts, didn't he, Kelsey?"

She wondered stupidly whether she was blushing, too, and putting one numb hand to her face, decided she must not be. Her cheeks felt cold, as if no blood coursed through them. She must be as white as alabaster.

But pale with horror or red with shame—it was all the same to Brandon, who couldn't see either one of them. It was as irrelevant as the difference between a starry sky and one of jungle black. She stared at the bandages that covered his eyes. There was so much he couldn't see, she thought in a fog of confusion, so much he didn't understand.

"Well, now," her father was saying, struggling for a dignified tone, "Douglas and I did have some dealings—"

"I'm asking Kelsey," Brandon said, giving each word a separate, chilling emphasis. "Did Douglas pay them?"

"Yes," she said quietly, staring just beyond his head to the picture window. Funny how everything had changed. Clouds must have rolled in, burying the stars. The night trees were no longer polished in silver. Now they were just a dirty, smoky gray, their leaves hanging limply from the branches as if exhausted.

But, she reminded herself, they were still the same trees. The difference was only a trick of the light, an illusion.

"Yes," she said more firmly, bringing her gaze back to him. She was still the same, too. Only Brandon's perceptions had changed, now that the cloud of the past had again rolled between them. "He paid them."

"How many?" His lips were so rigid they seemed immobile. "How much?"

"Seventeen thousand dollars," she said, proud of her voice for not faltering. Her father was sinking into his chair, like a leaking balloon, not looking at either of them. He hated hearing it put into a cold, immutable figure, she knew. He would have answered with some slippery generalization—"not too much," or "a few thousand." Or worse, he would have lied.

Uncomfortably she admitted to herself that she was lying, too, in a way. Though seventeen thousand dollars was exactly, to the penny, what Douglas had paid to impatient bookies on her father's behalf, she was deliberately leaving out the twenty-five thousand dollars her father had taken from the cash box.

A lie of omission. But a lie nonetheless.

She just didn't have the courage to tell Brandon about it. In spite of what had happened in the garden—and her lips still tingled—she couldn't. What happened out there had been about sex. It had nothing to do with whether he liked her. Or trusted her. Or believed a word she told him.

"Seventeen thousand dollars." Brandon repeated the words slowly, as if tasting each syllable separately. The curl of his lips told her the taste was bitter. "You're an expensive lady."

Kelsey's hands froze on the arms of the chair, and she sat very still. But her outward calm was only a thin facade. In her breast something wild and angry she hadn't even known was there began to churn. This was, finally, too much. Too much to endure in silence. Even her father made a small sound of indignation.

"Brandon! I know you probably didn't mean to be offensive—" her father sputtered, but Brandon's sharp tone sliced through it like a razor through a telephone cord. One second her father was a stream of defensive noises; the next, he was silent.

"*Very* expensive," Brandon said, his voice as cold as frozen steel. "And from what I saw, he got damn little for his money."

That did it. The tiny hurricane of resentment was released, and she shot to her feet.

"Your brother got every single thing he wanted," she said, and her voice was as full of furious heat as Brandon's had been full of ice. "He got power. He got control. He got a malicious sense of superiority." She ticked off the list acidly. "And, most of all, he got the sick thrill of watching us squirm."

Brandon didn't speak, but a nerve jumped in his jaw, and his hands closed over the rim of the desk in a white-knuckled grip.

"But you were talking about sex, weren't you, Brandon? You think your brother was breaking his heart wanting to get in bed with me." From the corner of her eye, she saw her father's outstretched hand, a reflexive gesture to try to stem her flood of anger, but she ignored it. Her mind was entirely focused on Brandon, who sat as rigid and still as a statue, his face turned toward her as if he could see through the bandages.

"Well, you're right. He *did* want to sleep with me. But it wasn't because he loved me—it was because he wanted to *own* me in every possible way. And if I chose to withhold that part of myself, if I refused to surrender every shred of personal dignity so that your brother could relish being my master, then that was my right."

Her voice had lowered to a fierce contralto. "And that's all I'm ever going to say to you about it, Brandon. You once told me never to mention Douglas to you again. Well, now I'm telling you—don't *ever* mention him to *me* again. It was my decision. Mine alone." She slowed down for emphasis. "It is none of your business."

He sat unmoving through her tirade, but finally one corner of his tight mouth tilted, in a parody of a smile. "What about the five thousand your father owes now? Whose business is that?"

Her heart thudded in her ears. "It's mine."

Again she sensed her father's nervous twitch. "But, Kelsey, you don't *have* five thous—"

She didn't look at him. "I'll get it," she said through clenched teeth, willing him to hush. Her hands were clenched, too, at her sides. Her arms ached up to her shoulders.

Brandon leaned forward. "Maybe you could sell that vulgar rock you called an engagement ring." His lips were now white and thin. "Unless you already have. I couldn't help noticing you aren't wearing it anymore."

Instinctively, she rubbed her bare ring finger, remembering how Brandon's hands had explored hers in the garden. The memory brought a physical pain, a rough touch against a raw wound.

"It's in your desk," she said, and the pain was like a low throb in her voice. "I'll never touch it again as long as I live. You're right. It *was* vulgar, just as Douglas was vulgar." She felt her insides begin to shake. "Just as you're vulgar, Brandon, when you say things like that to me."

He didn't speak. On trembling legs she somehow got all the way to the door. Once there, she turned around stiffly.

"Funny," she said, and though the shaking had finally reached her voice she was too angry to be embarrassed. "I thought taking his place would be difficult for you, but I was wrong. You're just like him, aren't you?"

HE COULDN'T FIGURE OUT why the hell it bothered him so much.

It was only a cheap insult. Why should it keep him tossing and turning all night? It was merely a transparent effort to deflect his criticisms by going on the offensive. Why should it have lodged in his brain like a poisoned dart, disrupting his concentration so that every thought led to the same mocking phrase—*You're just like him . . . you're just like him . . .*

He jammed his shirt into his trousers, then thrust one of the buttons on his cuffs through its hole so violently that it broke off and clattered away on the hardwood floor. He didn't even try to find it. He'd be damned if he'd end up on his hands and knees, groping about for a blasted button that had probably rolled under the bed simply to vex him. And all because she had tossed that last nasty barb. *You're just like him.*

He cursed as he tore off the ruined shirt and felt his way to the closet to get another. Why was he even thinking about it now? In one hour he'd be at Dr. James's office and these godforsaken bandages would finally be ripped away. He should be jubilant. He should be laughing, dancing, screaming from the rooftop. He was going to be a whole man again.

Instead, his mind was busy having a stupid, sophomoric argument with Kelsey Whittaker. There's nothing wrong with being like Douglas, his internal defense attorney contended, and then did a logical flip-flop, insisting he wasn't a bit like Douglas. He listed Douglas's good qualities and then, irrationally, trotted out all the ways in which he, Brandon, was different and better.

And on and on. It was pointless. It was exhausting.

His shirt now properly adjusted, he felt for the edge of the bed and sank onto it gratefully, eager to rest his leg. Getting the trousers and socks on had been a real ordeal—the damn leg still didn't want to bend. He poked with his good foot, locating the shoes that Frances had placed neatly within reach before she exited to give him some privacy.

One hour. And then he'd show Kelsey—

A discreet rap on the door interrupted him before he could complete the strange thought. Show Kelsey what?

"Mr. Brandon?" Frances's infallible radar must have told her he was finished dressing. "May I come in? Package for you."

He frowned and dug his bad foot into the shoe, trying not to make any sound, though the pain from his knee shot up to his hip. "Sure." He heard the door open. "What package?"

Frances made heavy breathing noises as she moved slowly into the room. It must be a very heavy package. It pained him not to be able to offer to help. "You should have let Greg bring it up, Frances," he said gruffly. "You're going to hurt yourself."

"Poof," she said with a groan as the package thudded against a wooden surface—probably the desk in the adjacent office. "I used to lug you up those stairs when you were a boy, and you weighed a lot more than this box." Her voice, still out of breath, came closer. "It's from a Mr. Fuller, and the darn thing must be full of bricks. It's as heavy as steel."

"Lead," he corrected automatically, as she expected him to, but his mind was racing. From Fuller? "What time is it?"

"Almost noon. Time for you to get going, unless you want to miss this appointment." He could hear the teasing smile in her voice. "Of course, if you're in no hurry, I'm sure the doctor could always reschedule you for sometime next week."

"The hell he will," Brandon said with a smile of his own. So Fuller had turned over the files, and just in the nick of time, too. Thank God. Brandon would have hated to have to talk to the lawyer about it. He hated the thought of telling anyone what Douglas had done.

You're just like him. Suddenly, with those dirty files on his desk, it was unendurable that Kelsey should think so. And, with a searing flash of insight, he knew why her insult was haunting him so. Ironically, she'd come to understand Douglas better than Brandon, his own brother, understood him. She had known long before Brandon did that Douglas had changed. She'd been here to watch the twisting of Douglas's personality. Brandon, as Fuller had said, had spent too long in the jungle.

He wondered exactly how she knew that Douglas had this dark side, this penchant for probing other people's secrets and making cruel use of them. Her father's, perhaps? Or did she have some secret of her own?

Whatever it was, Kelsey despised Douglas for it. She couldn't have faked the total contempt in her voice. Just as Brandon had easily identified her lies, now he recognized the truth when he heard it.

But the insight seemed only to lead him in further maddening circles. If she hated Douglas so, why had she agreed to marry him? Had it just been to provide financial security for her father? That didn't quite add up. Would a woman like Kelsey really be willing to throw her own happiness away to keep Tim Whittaker in gambling money?

He made fists with both hands and dug them into the soft mattress. It was time to make Kelsey answer some questions. He had been afraid, somehow, to press her. Afraid that she would continue to lie to him. Or that she would tell him the truth.

But now he saw quite clearly that they couldn't go on like this. He'd been attracted to her before Douglas died, and he was attracted to her now. But the future held nothing for them unless they set the past to rest—nothing but a long emotional siege of doubt and suspicion, resentment and bitterness. With a few starlit kisses thrown in, of course, just to keep them thoroughly miserable and off balance.

They had to talk. He was strong enough now to force the truth out of her—and to face it himself. As soon as he could see again . . .

"Frances, do me a favor?" He held out his hand, and Frances took it immediately.

"Anything," she said. "Except lug that box another inch."

"Tell Kelsey I want her to drive me to the doctor's office."

She hesitated, then squeezed his hand. "Now *that* I'll do with pleasure," she said, her voice curiously thick.

"She may not want to," he said tentatively, unsure how much Frances had ever overheard or simply guessed. "Her big meeting with Mr. Farnham is today, so she may not have time to—"

"That meeting's not until later this afternoon," Frances broke in impatiently, obviously unwilling to abandon the idea now. "You'll be home long before that. Oh, yes, I think she can be talked into it," she finished airily, a chuckle in her voice. "Ginny and I have her wrapped around our thumbs."

Smiling, he gripped her hand. "You like her, don't you?"

"Of course I do." The housekeeper heaved a great sigh, as though he were a dim-witted child. "I dote on her, you fool. Everybody who knows her does. I'd think that you, of all people, would remember that."

He caught his breath and wished desperately that he could see Frances's intelligent eyes, the better to read what she was implying. He, of all people... "*Everybody* does?"

"Well," she said carefully, "Douglas may not have. He wanted her, all right. But he wasn't really the doting type, not these past few years, anyway." She sighed again. "But other than that, yes, I think I can safely say *everybody*."

So his own feelings for her had been that obvious. For the first time, he felt embarrassed, as well as guilty. Douglas, Fuller, Frances... Hell, had everybody in California known? He thought he'd been so damn discreet!

"Tell me," he said, his voice not his own. "How do you think Douglas felt about...everybody else? Did he mind?"

There was a long silence, in which he knew Frances was trying to think of the right words. She would never lie to him, but she would want to present the truth in the least hurtful way.

"Yes, I believe he did mind," she said slowly, apparently forgetting for a moment that she was supposed to have trouble with English and lapsing into the eloquence of heartfelt conviction. "But not the way you're thinking. He minded the way a hunter would mind if you let a deer escape his sights. You know? The way a cat would mind if you took a sparrow from between its teeth."

She put her other hand over his. "I know that hurts," she said softly, and he could feel her gaze boring into him. "But you have to remember this. His minding didn't make it wrong."

And then, before he could even decide whether to admit he understood her, she left him. In the silence she left behind, he held on to the bedpost, feeling himself suddenly drowning in a flood of emotions, surrounded by images of frightened-doe eyes and sparrow-brown helplessness.

KELSEY WAS STILL ANGRY. Though she was scrupulously polite, he'd overheard the small, sharp stalactites of ice dripping from her voice when she told Frances that, yes, she would drive him to his appointment.

And now, as she perched on the chair next to his in Dr. James's crowded waiting room, she didn't lean back. She merely picked up a magazine and turned the pages with a crisp, rhythmic sound that proved she wasn't reading a single word.

He could picture her. Her long hair would fall halfway down her back, tickling her stiffened spine. Or maybe it would tumble over her shoulder as she bent, pretending to read. He had to grip the arm of his chair to keep from reaching over to find out. Damn these bandages.

Thankfully, Ginny's excited chattering on the other side of him more than compensated for Kelsey's frigid silence. Ginny had insisted on coming with them, and Kelsey and Brandon, perhaps both realizing they could use a buffer, had agreed.

"I want to be the first person you see," Ginny was saying now, jiggling in her seat so energetically that his own was rocking, too. "Or anyway the second. I know you have to look at Dr. James. But don't look at the nurse or anybody else, okay? That way I can be the first *girl* you see. Promise?"

"I promise, pesky," he said in his best world-weary voice, though he felt a warm pleasure at the thought of once again seeing her freckled face, a face that held so much intelligence and individuality. "Now for God's sake stop bouncing and babbling."

She settled down demurely, but he knew it wouldn't last. And, in a way, he was glad for her incessant noise, because it prevented him from agonizing about the next few, critical moments. He'd played the scene in his mind a thousand times. He would walk into James's office as if this was any ordinary visit, and then James would bring out his blunt-ended scissors and snip away the gauze. And then . . .

And then he would see. He would open his eyes, and he would see everything—the framed diplomas, the clear glass jarful of cotton balls and the doctor's own cottony head of curls.

And he'd see, for the first time in weeks, his own face.

Or what was left of it. Most of the cuts had been superficial—they were already practically healed, just slightly itchy, rough lines across his forehead. But not all. He knew there was a much deeper, very long cut that followed the line of his cheekbone, and one that had sliced through his right eyebrow. He knew it was bad because it hurt like hell, but he'd been too proud to ask whether it had made him a monster.

Now he would be able to see for himself.

See. He could hardly *think* the word without his heart racing. For a couple of days now, even through the bandages, he had been able to perceive light and shadow. James had said only that it was a good sign, a sign that the blood was resolving itself, draining away where it belonged. Brandon had read a promise into it: He was going to be able to see perfectly.

But even while his mind kept obediently chanting that positive thinker's mantra, his gut was busy twisting itself into a knot. Suppose something went wrong? Suppose when James flicked away the bandages there was nothing but more darkness?

Oh, God... Terror squeezed him until his heart seemed to pound angrily on his chest, jarring his bruised ribs, and it hurt to try to take a deep breath. His mouth was dry and his upper lip felt damp. He had a sudden urge to pull the bandages off himself, like the acrophobic who jumps off the cliff rather than endure the fear of falling another instant.

Kelsey's magazine was suddenly silent, as if she had heard the catch in his breath and was listening intently, trying to decipher it. With great effort he forced himself to breathe normally again. After a fractional pause, her magazine pages returned to their metronome's beat.

But why didn't the nurse come to get him? They must have been here half an hour already. He thought of asking Kelsey what time it was, but he bit back the words. He couldn't be sure his voice would be perfectly level, and he hated the thought that she might suspect he'd been jousting with terror.

But, damn it, it was inhumane to make him wait here forever!

"Mr. Traherne?"

There it was—finally. The nurse's voice was professionally impersonal, but to him it sounded like a call to arms. He forced himself to rise casually, though his muscles were clenched so tight they could have catapulted him out of his seat.

Kelsey and Ginny were up in a flash, too, one on either side of him, seeing that he got to the nurse safely.

Ginny burbled with excitement, but Kelsey was quiet. He wouldn't have known she was there except for the light pressure on his arm.

Just before she released him to the nurse's guidance, Kelsey spoke. "Brandon," she said, and he turned his head toward the sound. "I just wanted to tell you..." She seemed uncertain, and her voice, though still cool, had a melted sound, as if the stalactites had lost their sharp edges. "I'm sure..."

She seemed unable to go on.

"Oh, yes, your tea leaves." He was surprised at how gentle his own voice sounded, surprised at how he could pull himself out of his own fear to comfort hers. "I'll bet they said everything was going to be fine, didn't they, Kelsey?" He knew the nurse was waiting—he could feel her impatient fingers on his other arm—but he couldn't leave Kelsey like this. "Didn't they?"

"Yes," she said. The icicles had completely melted, pooling in her voice like tears. "Yes. Everything is going to be fine."

"Good," he said, pressing his arm in, capturing her trembling hand briefly against the wall of his chest. "I'm starting to have great faith in those tea leaves of yours."

He knew she was confused, trying to reconcile the warmth she heard in his voice with his bitterness of yesterday. He was confused, too. He never knew what to think when he was around her. He felt strapped to an emotional seesaw that tossed him from guilt and resentment to intimacy and desire with no control over his own behavior.

Soon, he thought with a surge of fierce determination. Soon, whether she liked it or not, they would bring that wild, seesawing ride to a soul-jarring halt. It would be one or the other—anger or desire. But not both. Not anymore.

Soon. As soon as he could see her, as soon as he could read the expression in her eyes. Then, face-to-face, gaze to gaze, he would *make* her tell him the truth.

CHAPTER ELEVEN

SOMEWHERE, KELSEY THOUGHT, in the seventh level of hell, you had to wait like this. You had to sit calmly and pretend to read recipes for apple strudel while in another room someone else was deciding your destiny.

She glanced at her watch. It was taking so long. Was that good or bad? Or was it just part of the hell? You waited so long it broke your heart, and you had to keep sitting and reading and smiling and pretending.

Ginny made no pretenses. She hovered around the door that led to the examining rooms, returning to Kelsey only long enough to ask her what time it was, then dashing back to the door.

And so, naturally, it was Ginny who saw him first.

"Brandon!"

Her cry spilled into the room like golden glitter, an intense, sparkling distillation of happiness that made everyone look up and smile as she threw herself at her brother.

"Brandon!" Ginny clung to his waist, burying her face in his chest. Though her words had turned into sobs, they were still the sound of pure ecstasy. "You're okay!" At the sound of Ginny's voice, Kelsey had risen from her chair, and she stood there still, her numbed fingers squeezing the forgotten magazine against her chest.

She couldn't cry out, couldn't fling herself into Brandon's arms. She could only stand and watch.

The nurse who had walked out with him patted Ginny's back, and then traded understanding smiles with Brandon over the little girl's head. That simple exchange of glances sent a dizzying thrill of relief rocketing through Kelsey. It was true. It was really true. He could see.

She shut her eyes tightly and let a wordless prayer of thanks vibrate through her. His ordeal was over. Though he had never spoken a word of fear, she'd known he must have felt it. She had seen it in his quick anger, heard it in the insults that had found their way, so unnaturally, to his lips. She'd even known, somehow, that when he seemed angry with her, he was really angry with fate.

But now that the waiting, and perhaps even the anger, were over, she allowed herself to admit her most secret hope—that the sight of her would break the chains that shackled his memory.

She opened her eyes, which were damp with unexpressed emotion, and found herself looking into his.

With a low gasp, she caught her breath. He still had both arms wrapped around Ginny, but he'd lifted his head and was staring across the small room, right at Kelsey, and his eyes were so miraculously the same, yet so achingly different, that she could hardly bear to look into them.

The scar that ran through the outer edge of his right eyebrow gave him a wistful appearance, where once there had been only a blithe symmetry. And there were new lines at the corners, lines that said he had, over the past long weeks, forged a bitter relationship with pain.

She tried to smile. "I'm so happy for you," she said in a low voice that probably didn't carry far enough to be heard.

He didn't seem to be listening, anyway. His gaze had left her eyes and was raking across her face, from her forehead to her chin, as if he was searching for something. Perhaps, she thought, remembering the wispy cobweb of pale lines where her own cuts had healed, he was discovering minute changes in her, too.

Or perhaps... She flushed as hope flared hotly within her chest. Perhaps he was just trying to capture a firefly memory, trying to follow the path of her features back to the place where the lost hours could be found. She held her face steady for his inspection, willing him to remember.

His gaze dropped, slowly taking in her whole body with that same lightly frowning concentration. Tingling heat broke out wherever his gaze alighted, but still she forced herself to stand quietly and submit. *Yes!* her thoughts cried out. *Yes! You touched me there... and there...*

But just when his study had become so deep and searching it was almost too personal for such a public place, he seemed to give up. With a nearly imperceptible shake of his head, he lifted his eyes to her face.

"Let's go home, pesky," he said, tousling his sister's hair. "Are you ready, Kelsey?"

A fierce disappointment overwhelmed her. Even after that scorching study, his eyes held no spark of recognition, no depth of intimate knowledge. He still didn't remember.

Suddenly she didn't think she could stand it. She wanted to weep, or scream or slap him—anything to shock him out of this oblivion. She wanted to take his hands and press them against her face, forcing the memory into him. She wanted to cry out, to tell him everything, every detail, until somehow one of those details became a trigger, and the memories burst free.

But she didn't. She couldn't. Instead, she put the magazine down carefully and picked up her purse.

"Ready," she said with a smile that didn't seem to fit her lips, in a voice that sounded stupidly cheerful.

Finally Ginny lifted her face, though she didn't loosen her hold on Brandon's waist. "Oh, Kelsey," she said breathlessly, completely unaware of any irony. "Isn't it *wonder-ful?*"

SEVERAL HOURS LATER Brandon leaned back in Douglas's desk chair and took a breath that went all the way down to his hips. It was done. All the telephone calls he'd put off for days—calls to friends, co-workers, businessmen—had finally been made.

He scanned his list of names, partly to be sure he'd covered everyone and partly for the pure joy of reading. Of the hundreds of little deprivations his blindness had forced him to endure, he'd missed his books the most. Especially at night when, although he was exhausted from hours in the exercise room, his mind teemed with mocking black devils and he couldn't sleep.

What would he read tonight? In his mind he sifted through his bedside titles, luxuriating in the prospect.

His gaze fell absently on the huge stack of files that rose from the corner of the desk, and as if someone had jerked on his mental reins, his thoughts skidded to a halt. Who was he fooling? Right at the top of the teetering stack were three fat files that had Kelsey Whittaker's name on them. It wasn't likely that any novel could compete with the story that lay between these deceptively bland manila folders.

He shifted uncomfortably. Why couldn't he trust her? When he had first seen her today, back at the doctor's office, she'd been so beautiful it had hurt to look at her. Standing there, with her hands clutching a magazine to her breast, her brown hair spilling over her shoulders, she'd been even more gorgeous than he remembered.

And more innocent. Memory had somehow exaggerated her sensuality, made her more a siren and less an angel. Not that she wasn't sexy. His whole body had lurched slightly at the sight of her. But it wasn't a centerfold sexuality dependent on tight jeans or pouting red lips. It came from somewhere far below makeup and clothing, something in the essence of her that plucked at the essence of him.

Her eyes had been brimming with tears, which made them even bluer, more luminous. He'd almost reached out, caught by a desire to hold her the way he'd held Ginny, to let her tears fall safely onto his shirt while he stroked her silken hair.

Or maybe not like Ginny at all. He'd been unable to stop his gaze from traveling down her body, his mind in a bewildering turmoil from trying to reconcile the tender urge to protect with the sudden hungry need to possess.

But when he looked again into those blue eyes, something was wrong. She seemed... He tried to pin it down. Angry? No. More like...disappointed. The expression had baffled him. He had expected her to be happy at his good news—and, indeed, when he'd first came out, her face had been as tearfully joyous as Ginny's. So why disappointed?

Or was he reading the expression wrong? Had she seen the greedy passion in his gaze and been offended by it? He ran his hand through his hair, feeling the familiar sensation of impotent frustration he thought he'd left behind with the bandages. Damn it, he just couldn't figure her out. Sometimes everything was perfect, like last night in the garden. But sometimes...sometimes her reactions were slightly off, like a guitar string that has become subtly flat.

That was why he knew he would read the files. Tonight he would open those folders and try to piece the puzzle together.

A furtive rap on his door roused him, and grabbing Kelsey's files, he quickly limped into his bedroom and dropped them on the end table next to the armchair before answering the knock.

It was Tim Whittaker, right on time and obviously concerned that Kelsey would catch him. When Brandon had asked him to come, they'd agreed not to tell Kelsey, at least not yet.

Looking at the older man now, Brandon realized he had made a lot of mistaken assumptions last night. He'd never seen Kelsey's father before, and he'd imagined a scoundrel, the kind of man who oiled his hair and dressed in loud plaids, a man whose sharp nose was a perfect complement to his beady black eyes.

What a narrow-minded stereotype that had been! Brandon could see that, before his excesses had made their mark in mottled skin and sagging jowls, Kelsey's father must have been an extremely good-looking man. He dressed in dapper clothes, and his shock of wavy white hair would have looked almost patrician over a stronger face.

Brandon was especially surprised to see that Tim Whittaker's blue eyes, while puffy and bloodshot, were quite intelligent and even held a touch of Kelsey's sweetness, though none of her straightforward strength.

What a waste, Brandon thought with a stab of pity. Tim Whittaker had been meant for better things. Kelsey had once told him that her mother had died when she was a little girl; keeping Tim's addictions in check would have been a Herculean task even for a loving wife, but it was clearly far beyond the powers of a ten-year-old child.

It might be beyond Brandon's powers, too, but he had to try. He motioned Tim to a chair, then took the one behind the desk.

There was a short silence as the two men sized each other up. Tim wasn't as garrulous as he had been last night, Brandon noticed. Apparently he'd realized it would be better to show up for this appointment sober.

Finally Tim spoke, his voice low and guarded. "You said you wanted to talk about the money."

"Right." Brandon had worried about how to broach the subject, but had finally decided it was best to tackle it head-on. Tim didn't need more coddling. He needed a well-intentioned kick in the rear. "I'll offer you a deal."

Tensing, Tim squinted. "What kind of deal?"

"A good one, I think." Brandon reached into the desk drawer and extracted a sheet of paper on which he'd written several names. "I'll settle the five thousand dollars for you," he said in a neutral tone, "when you meet with one of these doctors."

He shoved the paper across the desk. Tim gave it a long look before picking it up, and as he read it, a deep furrow appeared between his bushy white eyebrows.

"A psychiatrist?" He glared at Brandon. "You want me to see a *shrink?*"

"Yes," Brandon said, still neutral, but firm. "Unless you start seeing one of those doctors, I won't pay a penny."

"Damn you!" His red face growing redder, Kelsey's father wadded up the paper in a furious fist. "I'm not mentally ill!"

"No. But your gambling and drinking are sicknesses, and you need a doctor's help. I think you know that."

"The hell I do!"

Brandon wasn't surprised. The psychiatrists had told him to expect resistance. "If you want my help, you have to go." He shrugged, tapping his pen on the desk. "It's that simple."

"Well, maybe I *don't* want it," Tim began defiantly. "Kelsey said she—"

The mention of Kelsey's name cut through Brandon's carefully contained neutrality, and he leaned forward, gripping the pen so hard his knuckles ached. "Listen, Whittaker," he broke in, stifling the urge to shake him. How could anyone be so self-centered? "I'm giving you the benefit of the doubt here by assuming that you really love Kelsey." Tim made a noise, but Brandon held up a silencing hand. Words, as the cliché went, were cheap. He wanted proof.

"So if you do," he went on, "you won't put her through that. I'm sure she'd find the money, one way or another, but at what cost? Do you really want her to hock her jewelry at a pawnshop? Do you want her to be saddled with high-interest loans from some unscrupulous lender?"

Brandon felt his ire rising with every passing second, as his own lecture began to bring the picture of Kelsey's life into sharp, ugly focus. Pawn her jewelry? That had probably been done long ago. He'd never seen her wear any, except for Douglas's engagement ring. She'd probably been in more pawnshops by the age of twenty-six than most women see in a lifetime. She'd been struggling to keep this drowning man afloat for years.

"For God's sake," Brandon ended with a barely controlled disgust, "these aren't her debts. They're yours. And *you* should make the sacrifices, Tim, not your daughter."

For a long moment Kelsey's father just stared at Brandon. Then he transferred his numbed gaze to the hands he held balled in his lap. Finally, opening his fists, he began to smooth out the crumpled paper, straightening it over the curve of his thigh. When he looked back at Brandon, his eyes were glistening.

"My little girl," he said, and his voice was husky. "You know her as a woman, Brandon, but I remember when she really was my little girl."

The raw emotion in the older man's voice moved Brandon, in spite of everything, and his anger fizzled out like a wet firecracker. This wasn't the phony sentimentality that had set his teeth on edge last night. This was real, helpless pain.

"Does that mean you'll go?" Brandon's voice was thick, too.

But the older man's thoughts seemed turned deeply inward. "You know," he said musingly, "your brother never insisted on any doctors before he helped me."

That didn't surprise Brandon, either. But, in a strange way, his very lack of surprise horrified him. Knowing what he now did about Douglas, Brandon could see that his brother probably had had no interest in helping Kelsey's father get better. Tim's sickness kept him docile and dependent, the perfect servile lackey. And, best of all, playing the benevolent savior must have enabled Douglas to keep Kelsey obedient and grateful. Suddenly Brandon felt a little sick.

"I'm not my brother," he said a shade too loudly.

"Everyone has always implied that if I just had the gumption I could pull myself up by my bootstraps." Tim brought his troubled gaze up to Brandon finally, and the sober sadness Brandon saw there shocked him. These years hadn't been easy for Kelsey's father, either, had they? "But I never could. No matter how bad it got. This time, when Kelsey...when Douglas..." He swallowed hard. "This time I thought I'd finally hit rock bottom. I thought maybe this time I *could* find the strength, but..."

He faltered and rubbed his hands roughly over his face.

Brandon cleared his throat. Giving in to his pity wouldn't do Tim any good, but he had to keep reminding himself of that. "You need help, Tim. You can't do it alone."

"I know." The older man spoke into his hands, and the sound was as sharply painful as broken glass. "I know."

"So does this mean you'll go?"

Kelsey's father lowered his hands. "Yes," he said, nodding slowly, and Brandon felt all his muscles unclench in blessed relief. "For her sake, I'll go."

After Tim left, Brandon was restless. There were so many things he should be doing, so much to catch up on, but he couldn't concentrate. He watched from the tower window as Tim's small car maneuvered its way down to Cliff Road, and breathed a sigh when it disappeared from sight without running into Kelsey, who should be returning any minute from her meeting with Farnham. She'd been in town with Farnham all afternoon looking at properties she'd scouted for his new office building. But she should be back by now, shouldn't she? He checked his watch, remembering to be grateful that he was able to do even that simple thing. Nearly eight. Nearly dark.

He hoped she'd hurry. The world looked set for a storm, and ever since the accident he felt uneasy about anyone traveling in the rain. Especially Kelsey.

So he stayed at the window, watching. A rising wind ruffled through the bed of snapdragons, then stroked its invisible hand over the long summer grass. The treetops whispered and fidgeted like nervous old maids, and the sky was thick and wet and silver, as if made of mercury.

He knew those signs. It was going to be a serious storm. And it was going to be soon. He clenched his jaw and tried to see farther down Cliff Road.

But this was ridiculous. Maybe she'd decided to wait out the storm in San Francisco. She wouldn't have felt the need to call and let him know. He wasn't her keeper.

He plopped back onto the desk chair and, seeking distraction, yanked open a drawer. Nothing but stationery and stamps. Didn't Douglas do any work around here? Brandon rolled the drawer shut roughly and tried the next one.

No, he wasn't Kelsey's keeper, and he wasn't her father's keeper, either. So why was he ready to shell out five thousand dollars to pay the man's gambling debts? Why was he so concerned that Tim get himself into therapy quickly, before Kelsey found out anything about it? She'd be furious, Brandon knew, to discover that he had interfered. She had made it perfectly clear last night that it was none of his business.

But he felt this obscure sense of responsibility, a sense that Douglas had not done right by Tim Whittaker, that he had found Tim's vulnerabilities too useful. If Brandon could just get Tim started in therapy, he'd feel better. He'd have balanced out Douglas's exploitation and let everyone go their separate ways with a clear conscience.

Except that he didn't *want* them to go their separate ways. He wanted to help Tim Whittaker because he wanted to help Kelsey. And he wanted to help Kelsey because...

Distressed by the direction of his thoughts, he tugged open another drawer with a vengeance, and all his mental processes ground to a stop. A small black velvet box sat incongruously atop the rubber bands and paper clips. Kelsey's engagement ring. Reaching in slowly, he pulled out the box and set it on the desk, where he stared at it without touching it, as if it were a bomb that might go off at the slightest vibration.

He didn't open it. He didn't have to. He knew exactly what it looked like. It looked big, it looked vulgar, and it brought back so many memories his heart felt crowded and confused.

It hadn't been sized quite right for her, or else she had lost a little weight. It had slid down her finger to her knuckle when she dropped her hand, and it had rolled down toward her little finger while she typed. It must have been uncomfortable, because she frequently took it off. Douglas hadn't liked that. When he came into a room, his eyes had always darted to her left hand immediately, and his question, "Where's your ring, Kelsey?" had been stern enough to make her flush guiltily and reach to slip it on again.

She never looked at Brandon while she put the ring on, as if she was being forced to do something dirty and hated for anyone to see her. Not that he'd wanted to look. Every time the diamond slid onto her finger, his heart had knocked in his throat with a maddened rhythm.

No wonder Douglas had guessed how Brandon felt about her. He must have been as subtle as a train wreck. But he hadn't been able to help himself. He hated that ring.

Impulsively he snatched it from the desk and stood up. He'd get rid of the damn thing in the morning—return it, sell it, give it away if he had to. Tonight he just wanted it out of his sight. Douglas had had a floor safe put in—very hush-hush, as Douglas loved things to be. Brandon was the only person he'd trusted with the combination. That was the perfect burial spot for this wretched piece of bad taste and paranoid possessiveness.

But when, hunched over the floorboard that hid the secret compartment, he spun the combination lock to the correct numbers and flipped it open, he found that Douglas had already buried something else in the safe. A single sheet of paper that, obviously, he found as valuable as any four-carat diamond.

Dazed, Brandon knelt there for a long time, holding the paper, until his bad knee began to ache horribly. Still he stared at the paper, somehow knowing that it was the biggest, most important puzzle piece of all.

If only he could figure out how it fit in.

CHAPTER TWELVE

IT HAD A CERTAIN poetic justice, she thought numbly. The rain was right to fall tonight. After all, it had been raining when the whole mess began, so why not tonight, too, when it all was coming to an end?

Just minutes ago the rain had been only a few fat, isolated drops, which had splattered onto her hair and shoulders as she darted into the house, cold and exhausted from her marathon meeting with Mr. Farnham.

But now, as she stood watching from the first-floor tower alcove, the drops fell faster and faster, as if choreographed by a madman, until they formed one continuous, shifting curtain of silver in front of the window.

Lightning flickered silently, turning the rain-curtain white, hinting at ghostly trees that danced to the same wild beat and briefly imprinting the pale reflection of a sad and tired face on the windowpane.

No one would ever have guessed that the owner of that face had just landed a million-dollar deal for her company. Or that the man she loved had just today been handed a miracle. It was easier, perhaps, to guess that her heart was breaking.

The wind gusted suddenly, driving the sheet of rain against the window. Goosebumps rose on her skin, and she rubbed at them. It was all over. She and the rain had come full circle. Her professional assignment, the winning of Mr. Farnham's project, was finished as of an hour ago. After reading her proposals and viewing the proposed properties, Mr. Farnham had made a surprisingly quick decision and signed the contracts, giving the lucrative job to ODC.

So, if he didn't intend to fire her, and she assumed he didn't, Brandon would expect her to hurry back to the city to coordinate the job. And why shouldn't she? She'd run out of excuses to stay here.

Now that he was well, Brandon didn't need her anymore. The bandages were off, and he could drive himself anywhere or navigate down any pier in San Francisco. He could feed himself egg drop soup three times a day if he wanted to.

She had done everything she could to demonstrate her loyalty to Brandon and his family. At work, she'd safely steered the company through its biggest deal ever. At home, she'd filled in as the maid, the chauffeur, the secretary—whatever was needed. And, through it all, she had been Ginny's confidante, calming her whispered fears, drying her frantic tears.

But it hadn't been enough. She had understood last night that Brandon's most profound blindness was that he couldn't really see her, Kelsey Whittaker—struggling daughter, competent assistant, everyday person. He had only a warped vision of her, a vision in which she was the evil siren who enslaved, abused and ultimately destroyed his brother. Everything she did he interpreted according to that vision. And then, last night, when her father had said those things...

Well, it had been the proof he'd been looking for, hadn't it? If her kisses and her kindnesses had made him wonder, even briefly, whether his vision might be skewed, her father's tawdry tale had focused things again. It was obvious—she and her father were a team, together bleeding Douglas dry.

Hot tears filled her eyes. Always, always it was her father. She loved him, ached for him, but how much would she have to give up for him?

"Kelsey?"

It was Frances's voice, and Kelsey answered without turning around. "Yes," she said quietly. "I'm in here."

"I'm glad I checked," Frances said with some surprise. "I didn't know if you were home yet. Phone's for you. It's your dad."

Her father. Oh, not now. Not now, please. Kelsey pressed both hands to her temples, trying to force back the waves of exhausted resentment that pounded there. *Oh, Dad,* she cried wearily. *What is it now?*

BRANDON COULDN'T KEEP his hands off the files.

He'd wanted to wait until much later, when he was sure everyone was asleep. He'd tried valiantly to distract himself. He'd taken a long shower, then, pulling on his thick robe against the chill night, had built a fire in the bedroom grate. He had poured himself a Scotch, his first drink since the accident. He'd even turned on the television, wondering if the pleasure of his newly returned vision might make the endless parade of macho cops and slick lawyers more interesting.

It didn't. Within minutes he had flicked it off and found himself sitting in the armchair by the fire, Scotch on the end table, files in hand. He just couldn't wait any longer.

With a sick thrill that was somewhere between excitement and dread, he opened the first one, but to his surprise the file held only photos. The written reports must be in one of the others. Slowly he picked up the topmost picture, and instantly his blood ran cold.

Who the hell had taken this thing? He stared at it, incredulous. Shot from the side, it showed Kelsey kneeling on a picnic blanket, unbuttoning her blouse. He was in front of her, bending to unknot her shirttails, which had been tied at her waist. The camera angle had eliminated Ginny from the picture, not to mention the dozens of other company employees who were milling all over the park. It had even, somehow, managed to catch Kelsey at a moment when her bathing suit was in shadow, when it looked as though she were wearing nothing beneath the soon-to-be-discarded shirt...

His hand tightened, crumpling one corner of the disgusting photograph. Somehow it managed to make that lighthearted scene seem dirty. His posture looked urging, insisting. Their faces were inches apart.

He flipped the picture over violently, only to be confronted with another, this one of the two of them floating beside the capsized sunfish. Their suits were hidden beneath the lapping water—and their bare shoulders suggested a nakedness that was clearly absurd. But his hand was on her neck, under her hair, and his face was wet and hungry.

Then Brandon came to the last photo, and as soon as he saw the splashes of pink and white and yellow he knew what it was going to be. His hand shook slightly as he pulled it from the stack, and his breath stopped in his throat.

The people in the picture were lying on a bed of flowers, and though they were fully dressed, it seemed obvious they were making love. The man straddled the woman with a desperate rigidity, and the woman touched his face with fingers he remembered had been trembling...

"Brandon? Brandon, are you awake?"

He lifted his head, realizing as she spoke that the low, rapid knocking was not, after all, his heart. Kelsey was here, at his bedroom door, and suddenly his lungs were filled to bursting with the sweet, rueful smell of snapdragons.

"Just a minute," he called, and placed the folder face-down on the floor. He hurried to the door as fast as his weak knee would allow him, afraid he'd perhaps imagined her voice, that it was just some dulcet echo that had lingered in his memory, waiting to be coaxed out by the lovers in the picture.

Ignoring the pain that sliced through his knee, he flung open the door and there she stood, looking so beautiful he could hardly speak. She must have just returned from Farnham's meeting, for she wore a suit—a long, draped jacket that fell loosely over a short, molded skirt.

"Hi," he managed, trying to stop gawking like a kid. But he did so love to see her like this, believing she had her sensuality safely under wraps, not realizing it was like trying to trap sunlight in a bottle.

"Hi," she answered, and her voice had a soft catch in it. "May I come in?" She reached up and nervously tucked a stray tendril of hair back into its knot, as if she wasn't sure he'd say yes.

"Of course," he said, stepping back. "Please, sit down." He gestured to the chair by the fire. "I'll pull on some jeans."

"No," she said quickly. "No, please, don't worry about it. I know it's late—you were probably already in bed."

With a guilty lurch, he thought of the files. "No," he said, "I wasn't quite." But he was glad she didn't feel uncomfortable talking to him in his robe. He would have hated to leave her alone in here with those pictures.

Something was making her uncomfortable, though, even if it wasn't his robe. She'd wandered over to the fire and now stood looking down into it, her hands locked in front of her just below chest level, the fingers rubbing absently over the knuckles, her mind seemingly a million miles away. The firelight played on her face, giving it the illusion of mobility.

"What is it, Kelsey?" He moved a little closer, close enough to feel the heat that rippled out from the sparking logs. "Is anything wrong? Did Farnham change his mind, after all?"

"No." Without turning around, she shook her head, and the firelight slid in and out of her brown hair. "No. He signed the papers. Everything was perfect."

"Good." He hadn't yet learned enough about the company to understand fully what the deal would mean to ODC, but he knew how hard Kelsey had worked on it, and he was happy for her. "What is it, then? What's the matter?"

She took a long breath, as if she had to steady something deep inside her before she could answer. "It's my father," she said quietly. "I've just had a call from my father."

Oh, God! Brandon saw a sudden flash of angry red. Damn the man! Tim had promised he wouldn't talk to Kelsey about this, not until the therapy was under way. And now, with one phone call, he'd ruined everything.

He moved behind her, taking her shoulders in his hands roughly. "Your father needs help desperately, Kelsey." He tightened his fingers. "This was the only way I could get him to agree. Please don't be angry."

"Angry?" She twisted in his arms and turned a face flushed by the fire up to his. Her eyes sparkled, as if they had trapped some of the flames inside. "I'm not angry, Brandon. I'm—" She broke off, her eyes searching his face as though the word she needed was written somewhere on his features. "I'm grateful. I'm so grateful I don't even know what to say. He's really going to go through with it. He's already made an appointment with one of the doctors."

Her voice fractured. "I can't let you pay the note, of course—but that you were able to get him to see a doctor, when he has always rejected the idea from me...." Her eyes filled with tears. "Oh, Brandon, if you only knew what it means to me. I...I've been alone with this so long."

A primitive flood of protective energy rushed through him. His grip tightened and he pulled her closer, until her face was only inches from his and his knotted belt was crushed between them.

"Not anymore, sweetheart. You're not alone anymore."

Her face was tilted toward his, her eyes wide and trusting, her flushed cheeks warm, her lips so close he could feel each soft exhalation against his chin. It was a face he could drown in, a face full of promises, full of his most erotic fantasies and his most comforting dreams.

And she was *his*. She was like warm wax in his arms, melting against him, into him, through him. He lowered his lips, giving in to the need that thundered along his veins. She was his, and he would not, could not, stop himself from claiming his reward.

But before he reached her mouth, she spoke. "Thank you," she whispered, her voice trembling, her fingers clutching at his robe. And again, like a prayer. "Oh, thank you."

The words were like a knife driven upward through his gut, and he drew back just in time, staring in horror at her soft lips, parted like a sweet offering. What was he doing? Had this hot, hard need for her driven him quite mad?

How, he asked himself ruthlessly, was this different from what Douglas had done? Just like his brother, he had found Kelsey's needy places. And now he was going to take advantage of her gratitude. He was going to turn it into kisses and from there into touches, and from there—

No. He forced himself to release her shoulders, though his hands dropped to his sides with the heavy pain of deadweight. He wouldn't let himself become like Douglas.

"You're welcome," he said in a voice that sounded raw as it forced its way through his tight throat. "My pleasure."

"Brandon..." She seemed bewildered by his abrupt withdrawal, and she touched her warm hand to his chest, letting it rest on the bare skin exposed by the parted robe.

The simple touch burned like an ember from the fire. He wrenched away, twisting without regard for his knee, which flamed with pain and then, as if the muscles had torn loose from his control, buckled under him. With a low cry, she caught his arm and kept him from going down.

"Brandon!" she breathed, her face pale. "You're hurt."

He tried to free himself, reaching for the back of the chair for balance, but the pain was too great. He could not stand without her, and he felt perspiration bead his forehead. "I'm fine," he said through teeth that would not open.

But she wasn't fooled. "I'm going to help you to the bed," she said resolutely. "Can you walk if you lean on me?"

Without waiting for an answer, she tucked her shoulder under his arm and took a step. The motion rocked him forward, and he had no choice but to follow. The pain was subsiding, just a little, and finally he made it to the bed. Though he resisted, she eased him down, pressing his shoulders back so that he stretched out, propped against the pillows. Then she knelt beside the bed to lift his injured knee onto the mattress.

Oh, yes, that was better. A sigh of relief heaved through him as the pain receded like a cruel wave from a battered shore. He threw one arm across his forehead, letting the thick terry absorb the dampness there.

"I'm sorry. I thought my leg was stronger than that."

"You have to give it more time," she said softly, and without warning he felt her fingers feather across his knee. Their touch was cool over the lingering burn of pain, and he sighed involuntarily again. Her fingers halted at the sound. "Does it hurt when I touch it?"

He shook his head, not removing his arm from his eyes, not wanting to admit how much he needed that comforting touch. "No," he said. "It's very soothing."

And so she began again, a gentle, slow stroking, circling his kneecap, then sliding lightly into the sensitive hollow behind. Then up again to where the long thigh muscle met the knee. That felt good, too. Every inch of his leg ached from holding himself so unnaturally, favoring the knee when he walked. Pride had made him put away the crutch too soon.

He heard her shift, as if to settle herself more comfortably on her knees, and then she placed both hands on his leg. She started near his foot, with one palm on either side of his calf and, with just the barest pressure, stroked upward with her thumbs, massaging the muscles from ankle to thigh.

Up and down, soothing and gentling, drawing the pain out of him and filling him again with something quite intoxicating. It was heavenly, and he felt himself drifting, bewitched by the rhythmic magic of her fingers.

Lost in the trance, he couldn't have said exactly when the touch changed. At first it was too subtle to be sure, just the idea that her fingers were going a fraction of an inch higher with each stroke. And then he realized that her hands were no longer relaxing him, kneading his muscles into a supple quiescence. Instead, they were tightening as they touched, trailing tension in their wake. His body knew even before his mind made sense of it. She had, with those deft, exploring fingers, teased him to an iron-tense awareness of desire.

There was no hope of dissimulation. The robe was thick, but it didn't offer him camouflage enough. Perhaps, in the presence of such intensity, nothing would have.

And yet she didn't stop, as if she'd known all along what she was doing, as if she'd been doing it deliberately. He heard himself groan as her fingers kept traveling, as they found the upper edge of his thigh, and then the thrusting bone of his hip—and then brushed between his legs, daring to skim across the very heart of the fire.

"Kelsey," he murmured, strangled. "Kelsey, what are you doing?"

She let her fingers drift away, and he heard the rustle of the soft fabric of her suit as she stood up. Though his arm was still over his eyes, he could sense the change in light as she flicked off the overhead chandelier. The room seemed at once softer, darker and wilder, alive with the flickering shadows of the fire.

He heard her come back to the bed and then nothing—just a scent of lilac and a rustle of silky cloth. Finally, unable to bear not knowing, he took his arm from his eyes and looked at her.

Her jacket was gone, and her arms were raised as she worked to unhook the top of her blouse. His breath was the only sound in the room, and it was frantic, shallow, as if he struggled against an unseen antagonist. His own conscience, perhaps?

But then her blouse and skirt fell away, and her pale skin glowed in the dancing firelight. "Kelsey," he tried again, though he managed only a rough whisper. "What are you doing?"

He thought he saw her smile, though it might have been a trick of the shadows.

"I'm going to make love to you," she said softly, and came to the foot of the bed. Careful of his injured knee, she eased herself between his legs and ran one hand slowly up each of his thighs, which were rock hard with the wild tension of anticipation. This time her hands stopped before they met at the dark center of him. "Is that all right?"

Her tone was almost teasing, and he knew why. It was an idiotic question. Her fingers were only an inch away from the incontrovertible answer, though they refused to come closer, refused to touch him, until he told her to.

He tried to hold back. "Why?" He could hardly speak. Passion was like a beast that robbed him of his breath. "Why?"

"Because I want to," she said, the playful tone dropping from her voice. She shivered, and he could see her nipples harden against the thin lace of her bra. "I *need* to."

"Because you're grateful?" He watched her face carefully, terrified that she might, by some rebellious muscle that refused to cooperate in a lie, let him see that he was right. What then? What would he do? Did he have the strength to turn away from this? "Is that why?"

"No." She sounded almost angry, and with a low sound she closed her hands around him. "No," she whispered fiercely, and he groaned again, lost.

"Does this feel like gratitude?" She stroked him, a long, smooth, rhythmic motion that seemed designed to drag his soul right out of his body. His heart raced, and his legs fell apart weakly, surrendering, as she lowered her head to meet her hands.

"Does this?" she asked, her breath hot against him. And finally, desperately, he shook his head. He didn't know what it was. He only knew he would die without it.

And then there were no more words, just the pain of too much pleasure as she loved him, as she learned him, tasted him, changed him, owned him. Everything in him strained toward her, toward her warm, loving lips and her knowing fingers. His blood raced like hot arrows toward the place where she knelt, and soon he would be merely an empty shell except where she gave him life.

He almost gave in to it. He almost let the stampeding blood carry him over the black cliffs into the empty vortex, but somehow he found the strength to hold himself back.

Digging his fingers into her hair, he pulled her head away from him. "It's not enough," he said, though the sight of her face, all luminous eyes and damp, swollen lips, made the words a lie. It *was* enough, just to see what it had done to her, to know that her blood was racing, too, racing toward a throbbing center that needed him. The thought almost sent him over the edge, and he shut his eyes, breathing deeply to stop the fall.

"I want more," he whispered as he found his balance, and knowing he had attained at least a temporary plateau, he opened his eyes again.

She was watching him, looking beautiful and bemused, as if she'd been lost in some place that had no words and wasn't sure what he was saying. He would have to show her.

With hurried fingers he unknotted his already loosened belt and shrugged out of his robe. Then, raising himself on one arm, he reached around to free the clasp of her bra.

"Take that off," he ordered softly. She let go of him reluctantly, and with pale fingers slid the straps down her arms. He tossed the bra onto the floor and ran his finger slowly inside the elastic of her silken panties. "Those, too."

For that she had to lean back, and he watched, his breath heavy, as the firelight played across her high, rounded breasts. Her nipples were the color of fireshadow, dark and faintly burning, and between her legs another shadow beckoned.

When she was naked, she instinctively reached for him again, but he caught her hands in his. "No," he said, tugging her up toward him. "I need more. We both do."

Even in the dimness her small blush was visible, and for one fiercely aching moment he wished to God he could ignore the pain, could make the torn muscles whole again and do everything for her.

But he couldn't. It would have to be like this. And he would make it right. If only she knew how beautiful she was in the firelight, how it caressed her, licking every curve and hollow, touching her with tongues of darkest flame.

As she tilted forward, he slipped his hands under her hips and lifted her to her knees. "Put your legs around me," he whispered, and slowly, one at a time, she obeyed, though she shut her eyes as if she couldn't meet his gaze. With his hands cupping the rounded curves of her hips, he urged her toward the perfect center, lifted again slightly and held her there, letting her get used to the feel of him, nudging her open with a slow, warm insistence.

And though she moaned softly and ducked her head, her body bloomed for him. He caught his breath as he lowered her gently onto him, almost undone by the sight of their two separate bodies, their two separate souls, sliding into one perfect union. She fit around him so tightly that he knew he'd better go slowly....

With a low groan he shifted his hips and spread her legs even farther, pressing her down until he touched the deepest core of her. She sighed softly, and a tear trickled down her cheek, the fire lending it the color of sweetest brandy.

He brushed the tear away with a slow finger. "Am I hurting you? Do you want to stop?"

She shook her head, though another tear followed. "No," she said in a voice he hardly recognized. "No, please."

"Then lean back," he whispered, bringing his hands up to her breasts. He traced the puckered nipples with his thumbs. "Put your hands behind you."

Again she did as she was told, leaning back so that she was completely open to him. For a selfish moment he only looked, unable to believe that she was really his, that this moment had finally come.

And then he began to touch her, to urge her toward her own dark and silent cliffs, from which they would soon fall together.

But not too soon. He made himself go slowly, taking everything he knew, everything he had ever experienced or ever imagined, and bringing it to the act of loving her.

It was so right, so amazingly natural to be touching her like this. He had no trouble reading the tiny physical signals that told him what she needed. He used her breath, which came ever faster, as his guide; her lips, which fell apart softly and murmured wild, meaningless noises; her hands, which held on to his thighs, tightening and tensing.

But most of all he let her body tell him. At first she seemed to be waiting, poised and motionless. And then she quivered slightly in a timeless tremble and arced as if in pain. Finally, something deep inside her began to pulse against him.

And then it was too late for calculation, and his hands fell away, forgetting their mission. His willpower scattered as the tiny waves began to shudder through her, breaking over him with a hot, rippling rhythm.

She cried out and let her head fall back as the waves grew wilder, pounding now, with hurricane force, along the helpless shore of him. He tossed his head and half heard himself groan. It was unbearable, this building, throbbing heat. Instinct dictated that he must move, that he must lift and drive and meet the waves. But he couldn't. Sweat broke out on his face as the pain pinned him to the bed, making him unable to release himself from the frantic, mounting torture.

"Kelsey." Though his lips moved, no sound came. But somehow she knew, and she took over where his injured body failed him. She placed her damp, trembling hands on his chest and, finding the rhythm that needs no tutelage, worked to set him free. As she rocked over him, her pebbled nipples grazing his, a hot, wet wave of fire swallowed him whole, and he exploded inside it into a million incandescent embers.

As the embers dimmed and sank, leaving them both weakly drifting, her head dropped against his chest. Her breath was warm against his skin.

If there was gratitude here, he thought dreamily as he stroked the silken dampness of her back, it was his for her. For her incredible sweetness. Her boundless generosity. And for waiting here, through all these angry days, for him to find himself again.

But somehow it didn't feel like gratitude.

He kissed the crown of her quiescent head and smiled into the darkness. It felt like love.

SHE AWOKE SOMETIME LATER—a minute or an hour, she couldn't tell which, for though the fire was low in the grate the storm outside had not abated at all. Easing herself from Brandon's embrace, careful not to wake him, she wrapped herself in his discarded robe and stood up.

Though her body was sated, she couldn't sleep anymore. Her heart was too full, her mind too crowded with fear and hope and disappointment and elation and... She paced to the window and stared out into the storm. Her heart felt like that curtain of rain, made of hundreds of emotions that fell with such thick confusion they could not be taken one by one and identified.

She was sure of only one thing. She was not sorry she'd made love to him. When she had come here tonight, she had come expressly for that. She had decided to do so as soon as she'd heard her father's story.

And what a story! Her father had been more honest with her than ever before. He had admitted that he couldn't cope with his problems alone, abandoning the show of bravado he'd hidden behind all these years. And in doing so, he'd seemed braver, stronger, more a real father than ever before. She had wept a little, in gratitude and relief. Brandon had accomplished this, and her soul had been overwhelmed by the kindness and the wisdom that had prompted it. Brandon was *not* Douglas, was nothing like Douglas. She hugged that knowledge to her heart. She had not been wrong to love him. The only challenge left was to make *him* remember that he had not been wrong to love her, either.

And that was when she'd realized there was still one hope left to her. Perhaps his body could embrace what his mind rejected. Perhaps, in the moment of complete abandon that lovemaking could offer them, the floodgates of memory would open, too. Perhaps, at the split second when their two bodies melted into one another, he would look at her and she would see the knowledge in his eyes.

Her heart twisted, thinking of her high hopes as she'd entered this room. She had really believed it might happen. But it hadn't. His eyes had been beautiful, dazed and shimmering with an all-consuming passion. But they had not held any sign of remembering. One lost tear had trailed down her cheek, marking the failure.

Now all she could do was wait. Eventually he would wake up, and then she'd learn whether this second night of love would be the bridge to carry them over the empty gulf of the forgotten first night and into the safety of the future.

She folded her hands across her stomach, feeling the small fluttering beat that lingered there, and allowed herself to hope that it could. This second night had been, for her at least, even more cataclysmic than the first, richer, deeper, more transmuting. Maybe it would be enough.

Restlessly, she turned to look back at him, impatient to know which it would be—advance or retreat. But he looked so peaceful, his face unmarred by any awareness of pain, that she couldn't bring herself to wake him.

She prowled the room, pacing from window to bed, praying and remembering, until she thought she'd go crazy. Finally she curled up in the chair near the dying fire and toyed with a glass of amber liquor he'd obviously not had time to drink.

And then something caught her eye. It was her own name, neatly typed across the label of a manila folder. Her fingers drifted down of their own volition and nudged it open.

Confidential Report on Kelsey Anne Whittaker, the title page said, and her eyes widened, horrified. The return address was Al Fuller's office in San Francisco. Her heart stopped, then thudded heavily in a new, miserable beat. Was that what Brandon had been doing there yesterday? Had she, like a good and loyal fool, driven him to a private detective's office so that he could pick up this report on her?

With shaking fingers, she took the file into her lap and began to read, not caring anymore that it wasn't really hers to read. Brandon might have commissioned it, but it wasn't *his.* You couldn't, just by paying for them, own the private details of another person's life.

But though she was intently, compulsively focused on the report, her agitated mental state made the reading slow. She hadn't gotten through a full page when she heard the small sound. She looked up numbly and saw Brandon standing just a few feet away. He'd pulled on a pair of jeans, and he was holding something in his hand. She tried to focus. A piece of paper...

Finally something in his posture, in his expression, broke through her own mental turmoil. She frowned, stunned. He was standing, feet planted apart in the classic pose of aggression. The muscles in his upper arms stood out rigidly as though he was prepared for battle. His face was made of stone.

"Is this what you're looking for?" He shook the piece of paper with crisp, barely contained anger. "Is this what you came in here for, Kelsey? Your father's goddamn IOU?"

She was bewildered. "*You* have it?" she asked, horrified. She had known, of course, that someday she would have to talk to him about it. But she'd hoped that she would have time enough to make things right between them first.

She hadn't, even in her blackest moments, thought the crisis could come so soon. She knew that Douglas wouldn't have left it lying around exposed, and she hadn't even begun to consider the possibility that Brandon might find it. After all, it was only this morning that he'd regained his vision.

"Yes," he said bitterly, "I have it. I know you must be disappointed, going through that whole—" he flicked the paper toward the rumpled bed "—*charade* just so you could try to find it before I did. And all for nothing." He narrowed his eyes. "Poor Kelsey. What a waste of truly fine acting."

As his unspeakable words sank in, her arms went limp, and the file scattered unnoticed to the floor, typed pages falling like leaves at her feet. She took a deliberate step closer to him, and then, with a cold and flaying contempt, she slapped him.

"You bastard."

He didn't wince, didn't touch his cheek, though she knew it hurt. She'd left the burning imprint of her fingers.

"I've listened to enough of your insults." Her voice was glacial with fury. "And now, for once, you're going to listen to me. I don't care if you don't believe me. I don't expect you to. But you're going to hear it, all of it, just this once."

He stared at her, returning ice for ice. "Go on."

"You think I'm responsible for your brother's death," she said, "and in a way you're right. I should never have agreed to marry him. But he used my father to get to me for years, ever since he first spotted me in the typing pool. At first he just gave Dad a job, hoping I would feel grateful. But then, when I wasn't grateful *enough,* he began to lend Dad money to gamble, so that no matter what I did I couldn't ever control the situation. Douglas was always there, so sympathetic, with a couple of grand for a really great deal with really great odds. And then, when my father was in so deep that the sharks had threatened to hurt him..."

She stumbled, the underlying horror cracking the ice, and her voice broke as she remembered. "To...to hurt him—and me. Then your brother knew he had us, and it was time to turn the screw. He gave my father twenty-five thousand dollars to hold over the weekend and deposit for him on Monday. In cash, Brandon. Think about it! To a man with my father's addictions, which Douglas knew so well? And twenty-five thousand—the exact amount he needed to call off the thugs?"

Brandon opened his mouth, but she cut into the first halting syllable. "No, you *will* listen. I know my father was ultimately responsible. He didn't *have* to take the money. But it was the cruelest, most deliberate trap I've ever seen, and I'll never forgive your brother for setting it. Of course, my father did walk right into it. And then Douglas came to me.''

She shivered and wrenched the robe more tightly around her shaking body. "He was going to send my father to jail, he said, unless I agreed to marry him. I should be flattered. No one else was likely to want to marry me, he said, not with my father always hanging around my neck like an albatross. Even my charms, he said, couldn't induce most men to take on a liability like that.'' Her voice was dull, lacking even the lustre of ice now. "My father wouldn't survive time in jail, he said. He was weak. The other men would prey on him...."

She shut her eyes, sick all over again at the memory. "So I agreed. For one whole month I tried to do it, tried to reconcile myself to being Douglas's wife. Then I met you.'' She opened her eyes again and turned her blurred gaze to him. "And I knew I couldn't go through with it. I just couldn't. I had, God help me, fallen in love with you, and I was willing to send my father to jail rather than marry any man but you.''

Brandon took a convulsive step forward, but Kelsey backed away before he could get near her.

"The night, Brandon, the night you've forgotten, you came to me, and I told you I'd broken my engagement. You knew why, because you felt it, too. It was ripping you apart with guilt, but you couldn't stop yourself. You kissed me. You—'' she caught back a sob ''—you touched me and you made love to me, and then, when it was over, you put me in your car and drove me away from here, from him. I think he knew. I think he had seen ... something. He must have passed us on the road that night, and he must have gone a little mad, because he came after us. He slammed into the back of your car and...''

She stopped trying to swallow down her convulsive shuddering. Brandon's face looked ashen in the gray, rainy half-light, and she wondered whether Dr. James might have been right, after all. Perhaps it was too cruel to tell him.

But she couldn't stop now. Maybe, in a way, she *wanted* to hurt him, as he had hurt her.

"And then he was killed, and your mind just couldn't live with the guilt. So you transferred it all to me. You woke up from your coma a different man, Brandon—cruel and unfair, full of anger toward me for having ruined your family."

She drew herself up and met his stricken gaze with all the dignity she could muster. "Well, I've had enough. I've accepted the guilt for as long as I can. I'll take my share," she said, barely aware that she was weeping soundlessly, "but I won't take yours, too."

And with that, she turned around and ran down the stairs, feeling along the banister as her tears and the sleeping darkness blinded her. Somehow she found her purse where she had left it in the tower room, and fumbling for the keys to her ridiculous little rental car, she ran out into the rain, just as she had done the night it all began.

CHAPTER THIRTEEN

FOR AN AGONIZED MOMENT Brandon merely stood there, as numb and disoriented as if he'd been dropped into another universe. A strange dizziness threatened to overcome him, and his whole body began to shake, from the innermost muscles to every inch of skin. Was it true? Could anyone have put her through so much? And not just Douglas—could *he* have done this to her, as well? Frantically, he tried to strike a match and light the black pit of memory.

And then he heard the angry roar of her car engine, the spitting spray as tires raced through deep puddles on the circular drive in front of the house. He choked back a wave of terrified nausea. She shouldn't be out there. It was too dangerous, too wet, too slippery. The cliff was too high, her emotions too jagged, her eyes too blind with tears.

Hobbling on aching legs down the stairs, he reached the door and flung it open just in time to see her headlights sweeping through the rain toward him. He had to stop her. His leg wouldn't hold him long, but the curve of the driveway would bring her past him. If he could only make it ten more feet . . .

He stumbled over the threshold and, somehow managing to stay erect, flung himself into the storm. Icy fingers of rain grabbed for his bare skin, plucking the warmth out of his body. But he was still moving, and if there was any kindness in heaven, he would be in the center of the driveway in time to stop her. His mind was losing its focus, but he knew one thing—she must not get as far as the cliff.

He was already there, his bare feet in deep, glacial puddles, his face running with liquid frost, when her car came through the curve, windshield wipers flailing furiously at the sheets of rain. Would she even see him, see his numb, gray face, his frantically outstretched hands?

She had to. She had to stop because he loved her, and he would not let her be hurt again.

As it had once before, time slowed. The headlights slipped slowly, strangely toward him, impaling him with twin beams of milky light. And right there, in the glare, in the slow-motion terror of those headlights, he finally remembered.

Everything.

SHE'D ALREADY DECIDED to stop before she saw him. The drenching rain had cooled her fury, and she saw how insane her flight was. More running, more rain, more disaster. She knew she couldn't go on. Enough tragedy had come from this ill-starred love of hers already.

So her foot was moving toward the brake even as she rounded the corner and her headlights picked out his drenched body in the path. What was he doing? He was too close.

She screamed, though perhaps it was only an inner scream, and she pumped the pedal with thoughtless violence, whipping the wheel wildly to the left.

But even as she felt the inevitable spin begin, she didn't quite feel afraid. Somehow she didn't care what happened, as long as the spiraling car didn't touch the man who stood so stupidly, so gallantly, in the road. She closed her eyes with that prayer and waited for the crash.

But tonight, for once, the fates were on her side. As the car left the driveway, completely out of her control, its tires dug into the mushy thickness of the sodden turf. The spin didn't have enough momentum to fight that muddy grip— she hadn't, thank God, been going very fast—and the car swung to a twirling stop.

The engine killed itself, and in the strange, ensuing, hissing silence, an uncontrollable shaking took over her body. She lowered her head to the steering wheel, her ears deafened by the pounding of her heart, and clung with both hands to the wheel as her tears began to fall. She didn't try to stop them. There was nowhere to run now, nowhere to hide.

And then Brandon was there. He tore open the door as if he would rip it from its hinges and, with frantic, grasping hands, pulled her from the car.

"Kelsey," he cried, dragging her up against him. "Oh, God, Kelsey. What have I done?"

She sagged against his cold chest, numbly registering that she had heard those words before. Only the last time they'd been subtly different. Before, he'd asked, "What have *we* done?" Just one, insignificant pronoun was different. But she lifted her rain-soaked face, suddenly daring to hope.

Her heart nearly stopped. His wonderful face was twisted with agony. His eyes were hollow and haunted, and he leaned against the car as if he might fall. His leg—how had he ever gotten here? she wondered. He must be in such pain.

"I'm sorry, Kelsey," he said breathlessly, his voice as twisted as his face. The rain slid between his lips, as if it tried to take his words away. "Oh, but it's nothing, it's worth nothing, to say that, is it?" He groaned and held her tighter. "But I am, my love. I am so very, very sorry."

She shut her eyes, letting the pounding in her breast retreat, letting the wonderful words find their way into her tightly clenched heart and begin to loosen it.

"Do you really believe me?" she asked slowly.

"Yes," he said. He wrapped his arms around her and held her as if afraid she would run, or simply disappear. "But more than that, my love. I remember."

She lifted her head, a sudden warmth streaking through the chill. Was it possible? She didn't dare believe. She'd allowed herself to hope so many times—when he awakened in the hospital, when he first came home, when he kissed her, when he could finally see her again, and then, cruelest of all disappointments, when he had entered her body and failed to recognize it.

"It's true," he whispered, and a sudden, strange smile shaped his lips into something wonderful, something she remembered from what seemed like another life. "I remember everything. Every incredible moment."

She looked at him dubiously, through lashes that twinkled with the last few, softer drops of rain. The storm was passing. He lifted her chin, and he must have recognized the doubt that still darkened her eyes.

"You don't believe me? Well, let me see if I can convince you." He smiled again. "You weren't as bold then as you were tonight, were you, sweetheart? Even though, if my memory is as good as I think it is, you were a bit tipsy. I seem to remember an empty bottle of wine...."

At that, she almost smiled, too, though she hardly believed she could still remember how. "You make it sound worse than it was. It wasn't *completely* empty—"

"And still, drunk as a skunk, you didn't want me. I had to practically tie you down, didn't I, just to get your attention?"

"Well," she said, her smile deepening and a blush flaming on her cold cheeks, "hardly—"

"Figuratively speaking, of course." His eyes were lighter now, as if whatever had been haunting him was slowly floating away with the storm clouds. "I remember kneeling behind you, and you were so determined to resist me. I had to do all the work, didn't I?''

"Tonight," she countered, "it was the other way around—"

"And all you had on," he went on, his voice thickening suspiciously as his hands roamed down her back, "was that bit of nothing that you call a robe."

She lifted a handful of his thick terry cloth, which was now so soggy with rain it weighed a ton. "It was a perfectly respectable robe," she teased, light-headed with happiness. "Not a suit of armor, I'll admit, like this."

Laughing, he ran his hands through her hair, fingering its heavy wetness away from her damp face. "Not quite armor. It didn't offer me much protection tonight, did it?" She shook her head, remembering, blushing again.

"Maybe that's because there is no way we can really hide from each other, Kelsey." His suddenly sober gaze burned into her. "Maybe there is no protection from a love like this."

"Brandon, I—"

He put a long forefinger across her lips. "Think about it before you say anything. I hurt you terribly. Can you ever forgive me?"

"Yes," she murmured, amazed at how little all the ugly days mattered now. "Yes."

"Oh, Kelsey," he said, his fingers suddenly urgent on her arms, "if you can forgive me, if you only will, I swear to you I'll never hurt you again."

She shook her head. "I guess you don't remember *quite* everything," she said, trailing her fingers down his chest, forcing the muscles to contract and ripple. "Don't you remember standing there that night, promising me that what happened in the flowers would never happen again?"

She let her hand stop where his belt would have been if he'd taken time to find one. "Just think," she finished, "what *that* promise would have been worth. I think Dad's bookie would say the odds were about a hundred to one against it."

He pulled her into him and took her face fiercely in his hands. "Marry me," he said, his voice heavy with returning passion. "I swear to you I'll make you happy." He kissed her forehead. "In the flowers, in the bedroom, in the rain..."

But the specter of her father, which she had raised in such innocent fun, was suddenly between them. Douglas had been right about one thing—few men would willingly take on that burden.

"Brandon, about my father—" she had to say the worst now, while she could talk at all "—what if he doesn't get better?"

"We'll help him, sweetheart. We made it through this, didn't we? Together we're strong enough to conquer anything. There's a magic between us, Kelsey, and we'll share that magic with him."

And somehow she believed him. Yes, there *was* magic. She felt it coursing through her now, filling her veins with love and hope and... and something even more wonderful, something that sparkled and quivered and melted her from the inside out, though the night was so cold.

"I love you," she said, incapable of any real eloquence, hoping her tone alone could tell him all the things she couldn't find words to say.

Apparently it did. With a triumphant laugh, he pulled her into his arms and lowered his mouth to hers.

"Then help your crippled fiancé back into the house," he said as their cold lips met with a promise of a scorching heat to come, "and let the magic begin."

POSTCARDS FROM EUROPE

HARLEQUIN PRESENTS®

Travel across Europe in 1994 with Harlequin Presents. Collect a new Postcards From Europe title each month!

Don't miss
THE BRUGES ENGAGEMENT
by Madeleine Ker
Harlequin Presents #1650

Available in May, wherever Harlequin Presents books are sold.

HPPFE5

Hi—

I'm in trouble—I'm engaged to Stuart, but I suddenly wish my relationship with Jan Breydel wasn't strictly business. Perhaps it's simply the fairy-tale setting of Bruges. Belgium is such a romantic country!

Love, Geraldine

Fifty red-blooded, white-hot, true-blue hunks
from every State in the Union!

Look for MEN MADE IN AMERICA! Written by some of
our most popular authors, these stories feature fifty of
the strongest, sexiest men, each from a different state in
the union!

Two titles available every other month at your favorite
retail outlet.

In May, look for:

LOVE BY PROXY by Diana Palmer (Illinois)
POSSIBLES by Lass Small (Indiana)

In July, look for:

KISS YESTERDAY GOODBYE by Leigh Michaels (Iowa)
A TIME TO KEEP by Curtiss Ann Matlock (Kansas)

You won't be able to resist MEN MADE IN AMERICA!

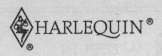

HARLEQUIN ®

Weddings, Inc.

Harlequin Books requests the pleasure of your company this June in Eternity, Massachusetts, for WEDDINGS, INC.

For generations, couples have been coming to Eternity, Massachusetts, to exchange wedding vows. Legend has it that those married in Eternity's chapel are destined for a lifetime of happiness. And the residents are more than willing to give the legend a hand.

Beginning in June, you can experience the legend of Eternity. Watch for one title per month, across all of the Harlequin series.

HARLEQUIN BOOKS... NOT THE SAME OLD STORY!

Relive the romance....
Harlequin is proud to bring you

A new collection of three complete novels every month. By the most requested authors, featuring the most requested themes.

Available in May:

Three handsome, successful, unmarried men are about to get the surprise of their lives.... Well, better late than never!

Three complete novels in one special collection:

DESIRE'S CHILD by Candace Schuler
INTO THE LIGHT by Judith Duncan
A SUMMER KIND OF LOVE by Shannon Waverly

Available at you're retail outlet from

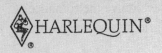

Harlequin proudly presents four stories about
convenient but not *conventional* reasons for marriage:

- ◆ To save your godchildren from a
  "wicked stepmother"

- ◆ To help out your eccentric aunt—and her sexy
  business partner

- ◆ To bring an old man happiness by making him
  a grandfather

- ◆ To escape from a ghostly existence and become a
  real woman

Marriage By Design—four brand-new stories by four
of Harlequin's most popular authors:

CATHY GILLEN THACKER
JASMINE CRESSWELL
GLENDA SANDERS
MARGARET CHITTENDEN

Don't miss this exciting collection of stories about
marriages of convenience. Available in April, wherever
Harlequin books are sold.

MBD94

HARLEQUIN®

Don't miss these Harlequin favorites by some of our most distinguished authors!
And now, you can receive a discount by ordering two or more titles!

HT #25551	THE OTHER WOMAN by Candace Schuler	$2.99	☐
HT #25539	FOOLS RUSH IN by Vicki Lewis Thompson	$2.99	☐
HP #11550	THE GOLDEN GREEK by Sally Wentworth	$2.89	☐
HP #11603	PAST ALL REASON by Kay Thorpe	$2.99	☐
HR #03228	MEANT FOR EACH OTHER by Rebecca Winters	$2.89	☐
HR #03268	THE BAD PENNY by Susan Fox	$2.99	☐
HS #70532	TOUCH THE DAWN by Karen Young	$3.39	☐
HS #70540	FOR THE LOVE OF IVY by Barbara Kaye	$3.39	☐
HI #22177	MINDGAME by Laura Pender	$2.79	☐
HI #22214	TO DIE FOR by M.J. Rodgers	$2.89	☐
HAR #16421	HAPPY NEW YEAR, DARLING by Margaret St. George	$3.29	☐
HAR #16507	THE UNEXPECTED GROOM by Muriel Jensen	$3.50	☐
HH #28774	SPINDRIFT by Miranda Jarrett	$3.99	☐
HH #28782	SWEET SENSATIONS by Julie Tetel	$3.99	☐

Harlequin Promotional Titles

#83259	UNTAMED MAVERICK HEARTS (Short-story collection featuring Heather Graham Pozzessere, Patricia Potter, Joan Johnston)	$4.99	☐

(limited quantities available on certain titles)

	AMOUNT	$
DEDUCT:	10% DISCOUNT FOR 2+ BOOKS	$
	POSTAGE & HANDLING	$
	($1.00 for one book, 50¢ for each additional)	
	APPLICABLE TAXES*	$ _____
	TOTAL PAYABLE	$ _____
	(check or money order—please do not send cash)	

To order, complete this form and send it, along with a check or money order for the total above, payable to Harlequin Books, to: **In the U.S.:** 3010 Walden Avenue, P.O. Box 9047, Buffalo, NY 14269-9047; **In Canada:** P.O. Box 613, Fort Erie, Ontario, L2A 5X3.

Name: _____

Address: _____ City: _____

State/Prov.: _____ Zip/Postal Code: _____

*New York residents remit applicable sales taxes.
Canadian residents remit applicable GST and provincial taxes.

HBACK-AJ